A CANDLELIGHT REGENCY

CANDLELIGHT ROMANCES

MASTER OF ROXTON

BY
Elisabeth Barr

A CANDLELIGHT REGENCY

Published by
Dell Publishing Co., Inc.
1 Dag Hammarskjold Plaza
New York, New York 10017

Originally published in Great Britain by
Robert Hale & Company
Copyright © 1973 by Elisabeth Barr

Dell ® TM 681510, Dell Publishing Co., Inc.
Printed in the United States of America
First U.S. printing—January 1976

CHAPTER ONE

It was a fine, clear morning in 1817 when the *Rose
Stuart* sailed splendidly into Sydney Harbour; Philip
York stood on board, and surveyed the thrusting,
bustling town sprawled at the water's edge. The ship,
her long journey from England over, was full of the
commotion of passengers making ready to disembark.
He had enjoyed the company of some of his fellow-
passengers: men going out to seek their fortunes in the
new Continent, where there was enough land for everyone; relatives joining those of their family who had already proved the theory that Australia was a land of
great opportunity. He had listened and not spoken
much, for he was a reserved man and had no desire to
talk of his own reasons for this voyage.

Quite a few feminine hearts on board had been
stirred at the sight of him. He was in his early thirties,
a tall man, who had fought under Wellington at Waterloo, only two years previously, and still bore a small,
puckered scar on his right cheek as a memento. His
dark eyes were sombre, his face aristocratic, with its
high-bridge, bony nose, his mouth full but firm and disciplined; above his lean face brown hair was thick, inclined to curl; he was a man of action, not talk, and he
was not entirely at ease in the company of women,
which fact they recognized and found delightful.

He had come with little luggage and no servant. Yes,
he was merely visiting Australia, he had replied reluctantly, in answer to the questions of a persistent,
middle-aged matron, mother of two marriageable
daughters. No, he imagined it would not be a long visit;
he had fended off further curious questions with a bow,
an inclination of his head, and moved discreetly away.

As soon as he was ashore, Philip went to a hotel in the busy main street, washed, ate a meal, and enquired the way to the Governor's office; then he hired a conveyance to take him there.

He could not see the Governor, he was told; he had no appointment. The harassed young clerk was helpful, though he pulled at his lower lip, and shook his head dubiously at Philip's request.

"Records of the convicts shipped out here? Why, sir, do you know how many they send us in a year? Enough, to be sure, to make a man suppose that England is overrun with criminals. There are convict camps, to which they are sent when they arrive. You have with you a free pardon, you say? I shall need to show it to the Governor, before I give you authority to ask for camp records. The convicts do not stay in the camps, sir, they are put to work. There is nothing like hard work to purge a man's soul of evil." He nodded virtuously, lips pursed; he prided himself on his Christian principles. "Road works, public buildings, convict labour for the settlers on the sheep farms; this man you seek could be working anywhere, hired out to farmer or builder, you understand."

Philip tried to imagine his cousin, Richard, as part of a road-working gang—and failed; but the thought of all that Richard must have endured since his transportation from England, two years previously, filled him with compassion.

He was intensely busy during the next few days; armed with his letter of authority, and the free pardon that he had brought from England, he made intensive search and enquiry for his cousin in convict camps round and about Sydney. There were times when he almost despaired, but he never gave up; at the end of a week, he had the information he wanted: a man named Richard Roxton had been sent as convict labour to a sheep station on the far side of the Blue Mountains, owned by a man called James Brandon, and called Taroola.

Philip hired a couple of horses; took only enough for his immediate needs, glad that he had travelled light; the Blue Mountains were forty miles to the north-west of Sydney. He rode out of Sydney, thankful that the formalities were over, and the journey to bring Richard home to England had begun.

He thought, as he rode, of his cousin, a few years younger than himself, the only child of the Baronet, Sir Thomas Roxton, and his wife, Eleanor. As a child and a young man, Richard had been indulged in every whim by his doting parents; he had been born when they were middle-aged, and was heir to Roxton Park. When he came of age, Richard's behaviour had begun to cause his parents some concern; Richard had kept his own establishment in London, but tales of his women, his gambling debts, his wild life there, had filtered back to the quiet West Country town where his parents lived; later, there were uglier tales; violence, robbery, smuggling, a rumour that Richard was part of the notorious gang that committed outrageous crimes; ending finally in the act that had led to life deportation. Had he been a poor man, had his father not fought with all the money and authority in his power in a vain attempt to prove his son innocent, then Richard would surely have been hanged. He had now, in fact, been proved innocent of robbery and assault, thanks to the confession of a dying man; and Philip hoped, with all his heart, that the events of the last two years had hardened Richard from a spoilt boy, into a man.

As he rode, he was continually astonished and delighted by the beauty of the scenery; and, as he neared the mountains, he marvelled at the tremendous grandeur of peaks that towered to the sky, and the beauty of the deep valleys, the ranges rolled away into hazy blue distances; everywhere, there were strange creatures such as he had never seen, and lush green vegetation that was, in itself, a promise of plenty. He looked at the huge trees towering above him, and felt dwarfed; in spite of his air of arrogance, his authoritative manner, he had a deep, inner humility. This would be a good country in which to begin a new life, he thought.

On the Western side of the river, he encountered the first of the settlers' huts; the settlers were friendly, thirsty for company, but he would not stay.

"I am going to Taroola," he told them. "Do you know of it?"

"Aye. James Brandon's place. A man who says he is going to make a fortune with sheep. That's as may be. . . ."

Philip passed a squatters' camp; the men were on their way west to find sheep runs. They were tanned, bearded men, sitting outside their roughly-made tents, drinking tea, without apparently a care in the world. They let him water his horses nearby, but they had never heard of Taroola; one of them admitted, frankly, that he was a convict who had served his time and added that he had no desire to return to England.

" 'Tis a fine place this," the man told him. "There's plenty in it for those as will work; enough for a man to eat, and a decent wage." He spat. "No Game Laws here to punish a man with transportation because he takes a rabbit so as his family don't go hungry."

Philip said nothing; the man looked carefree, and he thought about him, as he rode the last few miles towards Taroola. Richard and he had been lucky; but life was unjust to a man who had nothing, and came from working stock. He thought of the law that had been passed only the previous year, punishing a man found in possession of a net for taking rabbits by transporting him for seven years. He thought of the poverty and ignorance that was fouling the fair English countryside; well, there would be work enough for Richard, when he came home. Since his father's illness, and his mother's mental state, the farms and cottages had been mismanaged and neglected.

He rode beneath the majestic trees with their interlacing branches, and came out on a small, rough path that wound up to a gentle rise; on the other side of the rise, the squatters had told him, was Taroola. So Philip came upon it, in the heat of the day, a long, low building in a clearing by the river; a little distance from it stood a crop of outbuildings, wool-sheds no doubt, he thought, and accommodation for the men who worked on the station. All the buildings were clustered on a rounded, gentle hillock that sloped to a broad sash of water, and was backed by trees. The place seemed to be in good repair, well-fenced and tidy, and was of fair size. He could see a flock of sheep moving on the skyline, a man riding beside them on a horse; as he approached, another man came from one of the sheds, and crossed to a small wooden cabin in a clearing. He was tall, with thick, gingery hair, and heavy shoulders; he glanced incuriously at the visitor, called an unintelligible greeting and went on his way.

Philip tethered the horses at the fence in front of the house; and walked up to the open door; as he reached it, a woman came out, and stood looking at him, shading her eyes with her hand.

She was in her early twenties, he guessed; and she was very beautiful; tall, statuesque, in her fresh print dress, her head bare, her hair flowing unexpectedly loose over her shoulders, instead of being tidily dressed to her head. It was the most magnificent hair he had ever seen; a rich, dark red, like old, polished mahogany, hanging long and straight and thick to her waist. Her face was milky-skinned, unweathered by the hot Australian sun, her features clear-cut, her eyes dark-blue beneath smooth, arched brows. She neither moved nor spoke as he approached her, merely stood watching him gravely.

"Good-afternoon," he said courteously. "This is Taroola?"

"Yes." Her voice was unexpectedly cultured. She smiled and added:

"*I* am Taroola. The station is named after me."

"Surely you do not own it?" he exclaimed, astonished.

"No. It is my father's. If your business is with him, may I ask you to make it brief? He has been ill and has little strength, yet. It is a recurring fever that attacks him at intervals. If you promise not to tire him, then you are most welcome. We do not see many people, Mr.——?"

"My name is Philip York," he said. *Taroola,* he thought? What an extraordinary name for a young woman! He was used to women being soft, shy, self-effacing in their youth; formidable in middle-age, autocratic in their declining years. This woman was none of those things; she had an air of knowing her own mind and being able to conduct her own affairs that intrigued him.

"Have you ridden far?" she asked.

"From Sydney."

"Sydney!" She looked wistful for a moment and he wondered if she was thinking of shops that sold bonnets, ribbons and laces, and dainty, feminine things. "It seems like another world to me. I have not left this place for more than a year. Go into the house, and I will give instructions for your horses to be fed and watered."

She walked towards the outbuildings; she had a beautiful walk, he thought, slow, graceful, her head held high. He looked at her thoughtfully for a moment, before he went into the house.

It was surprisingly well-furnished; the furniture, old and solid, had obviously been imported from England, had been lovingly cared for and polished. There were skin rugs on the floor of the big room which he entered, shelves filled with books, a carved oak chest; there was a candelabra, very heavy, and obviously of silver, an astonishing thing to see in the Australian bush, he reflected. A table was laid for tea, with a fine linen cloth and delicate china, which also struck him as incongruous. By the table was a couch on which lay a man, his legs covered with a rug. He looked prematurely old, his skin dried and weatherbeaten; his thick hair was silver, his eyes tired, and the hands restlessly pulling at the fringe of the rug were thin-fingered and blue-veined; but he looked up, smiling with pleasure and surprise, when he saw Philip.

"I thought I heard voices! A visitor! Welcome, whoever you are. Apart from our own staff, we see no one but squatters passing through in search of grazing country, and occasionally the aborigines. You have met my daughter?"

"Yes," said Philip. "She is giving instructions for my horses to be attended to; she tells me that her name is Taroola. I have never heard so strange a name for a woman!"

The light-blue eyes were shrewd.

"But attractive, is it not? It sits on her better than the name by which she was christened—Anne. I am James Brandon."

"I am Philip York." He hesitated. "I am come upon business."

"I have no sheep to sell, neither do I wish to add to my flock. However, whatever your business, it will keep until we have had tea."

His voice was as educated as his daughter's; he did not fit the conventional pattern of immigrant at all, Philip thought, puzzled. At that moment, Taroola came into the room; he would never think of her as Anne, or, more correctly, Miss Brandon, Philip realized. The name her father called her sat magnificently upon her.

"I am sure Mr. York will be glad to wash the dust of the journey from his hands before we begin," she told her father.

She took Philip to a room as comfortably furnished as the rest of the house; brought him a pitcher of water, and thick, soft towels. He looked out of the window, at the lush land, drowsy under the sun that would grow unbearably hot as summer climbed towards its peak. He could hear the monotonous, mournful 'baa' of sheep in the distance, and other sounds of birds in the trees, strange to him, and utterly fascinating.

They were waiting when he returned; Taroola sat gracefully behind a silver teapot. She appeared to have little domestic help, though an elderly woman had brought hot water and food. It would not be an easy life for her, he thought, particularly with an ailing father.

"You are surprised," said James Brandon, with a sly smile, "to be served with English afternoon tea, in the Australian bush?"

"Yes," Philip admitted, with one of his rare smiles. "And delighted, I must confess."

"Have you lately come from England?" Taroola asked him.

"Yes. I arrived in Sydney less than two weeks ago."

James Brandon was eager to discuss the voyage and to talk about Australia; there was a great future, he said knowledgeably, in the wool and meat that Australia nurtured. Every year, more and more families crossed the road over the Blue Mountains in search of rich grazing land. There was plenty for everyone; it was a land of opportunity. He looked expectantly at Philip, who shook his head.

"When my business is done, I return to England," he said.

"A pity we cannot tempt him to stay, eh, Taroola?" James said to his daughter with light, dry humour. "There is a great deal still to be done here, Mr. York, room for many more flocks to graze. I have an excellent manager, but I am subject to bouts of fever, and it is then that I lie here and fret for the inactivity I am forced to endure."

Philip saw the look on Taroola's face, as well as on her father's, and he understood. A couple of sons were needed to run a place like this; James was an old man,

with only a daughter, who could never deputize for
him. His wife was dead; she had died soon after the
journey to Australia, he told Philip briefly, when
Taroola was a baby.

"And now, Mr. York, your business," Mr. Brandon
said briskly.

He had almost forgotten the object of his journey,
Philip realized.

"I understand that you employ a man named
Richard Roxton," he said.

There was silence; he saw the wariness and astonishment in James' face, the sudden leap of interest in the
blue eyes of his daughter.

"Yes," said James Brandon, slowly. "What of it?"

"He is—" Philip paused "—a convict."

"That is so," James replied precisely. "We employ
convict labour to supplement our own; it is good, bad,
and indifferent. And your interest in this man?"

"He is my cousin," Philip replied. "He was convicted
of robbery with violence, and deported. His associates
were unfortunately, men of doubtful reputation, and
so suspicion was cast upon him; he was wrongly accused, however, for the man who committed the crime
for which Richard was punished, confessed the truth
just before he died. I am here at the request of my
Uncle, Richard's father, to escort my cousin home. I
have the pardon, and the necessary letters of authority."

The silence seemed to grow deeper and more pro-
found. James looked completely taken aback; Taroola's
face fascinated Philip. Her smile was like the sunrise,
her eyes were full of joy.

"He is *not* a criminal, Father!" she whispered. "I
was sure that he could not be! Mr. York has brought a
pardon!"

The heavy grey brows came together over eyes that
were suddenly cold. Philip said courteously:

"Naturally, you will wish to see the papers I have

brought." But his eyes were on Taroola still; she looked radiant.

Taroola looked at her father; then, suddenly, she turned and went swiftly from the room, her head high. James Brandon lay back against his cushions as though he was exhausted.

"So," he said tiredly. "Richard Roxton is proved not guilty of the crime for which he is serving sentence and you have come to take him back to England. I regret that I have found him lazy, irresponsible, surly; the men do not like working with him. He has been at great pains to assure me that his background and up-bringing have fitted him for a vastly different life from the one he has here and he dislikes work of any kind."

Philip said quietly:

"No doubt resentment and a sense of injustice are responsible for his behaviour."

"I think not. You are his kin, and I respect your loyalty; he is, on his own admission, the only son of elderly parents, heir to money and possessions; it is my opinion that he has been over-indulged all his life. He is also a man capable of great charm when he chooses to exert it; and my daughter, a woman of good sense in other matters, has succumbed to this charm, as you see, and is quite enamoured of him. I keep a close watch upon my daughter, Mr. York—but I am glad you are to take your cousin home!"

"May I see him?" Philip asked.

"You will find him mending the fence on the far side of the last woolshed." James hesitated, and added candidly:

"I like you, Mr. York. I have known you little more than an hour; but my judgement of men has never been faulty. If Taroola's fancy had been for you, it would have received my blessing. I am an old man and I have no son to leave this place to; if Taroola married a man I could trust—" he shrugged and sighed; Philip coloured and said stiffly:

"I have roots in England, Mr. Brandon. And no desire at all to be wed."

The older man smiled; his voice was dry.

"How old are you? Thirty-two? I still think you will not die a bachelor, Mr. York. You will want to return to Sydney as soon as possible, no doubt."

"Yes. I have brought a spare horse with me."

"You must remain as my guest tonight." The voice was eager. He looked so ill that Philip felt moved to pity.

"Thank you," Philip said. "I should like to make an early start tomorrow."

The old face hardened for a moment. "Richard will not, I am sure, object to eating with the other men, as usual, on his last night here. I will see you later, Mr. York."

As Philip left the house, Taroola came towards him, walking with the lovely fluid grace he had so admired. There were traces of tears in her eyes, though she still looked happy.

"Would that I could give your news to Richard!" she said. "But for all my gladness, I am sorry you have come to take him from here!"

"Your father does not share that view!" Philip replied shortly.

"And you seem to agree with him!"

"I have known him since we were boys!" Philip said.

Her chin tilted defiantly.

"I find him most agreeable company!" she retorted. "Have you no compassion for a man falsely accused and made to suffer great hardship?"

"Yes," he replied equably. "And I am here to right that wrong."

She watched him walk in the direction of the out-buildings; he did not look back, and she thought scornfully: how stiff-necked, how arrogant he is! She thought of Richard's departure with intense pain; they had enjoyed little enough of one another's company, she thought. A few brief, stolen meetings, at the end of the day, always within call of the house. Glances, hands touching, whispered phrases, the memory of which could make the blood flow warmly in her cheeks.

Richard had his back to Philip, as the latter came towards him; he was leaning on the fence, staring moodily into space, his tools on the ground beside him. He has suffered a great deal, Philip reminded himself; knowing he was convicted unjustly must have made him bitter. Whatever his weaknesses, life has been hard for him since he was shipped out here.

"Richard!" he called.

Richard turned swiftly; he was thinner, Philip realized, his face harder, the mouth sullen and discontented. His fair hair shone almost silver-white in the sun; his light-grey eyes widened when he saw his cousin, and he looked amazed; but his voice was so mocking that Philip marvelled at his cool self-possession.

"*Well!* My dear cousin! And what has brought you here? Not concern for my welfare surely?"

Richard had always baited him, ever since they were children; Philip had merely retreated further and further behind a high wall of reserve, a fact that had always infuriated his cousin. Now he merely said calmly:

"Matthew Warby is dead. Before he died, he confessed that he had been responsible for the crime for which you were transported. Your father set in motion the necessary legal machinery to obtain a pardon for you, which I have with me; and he has sent me to bring you home."

Richard looked stunned and incredulous.

"Matthew Warby? *Confessed?* By Heaven, I don't believe it!"

"You can inspect the documents for yourself. We leave for Sydney early tomorrow morning," Philip replied.

Richard had always held his cousin in contempt; at that moment, he almost liked him. He drew a long, deep breath and looked around him.

"Free!" he cried exultantly. *"Free* to get out of this damned, God-forsaken place, to go back to a civilized society and decent living again! Old Warby *confessed!"* he threw his head back and laughed. "That is hard to believe!"

"He was dying. He sent for a magistrate, and your father, and made written confession, in order, he said, that he might die with a clear conscience."

Again Richard laughed.

"Your manner proclaims your disapproval as loudly as a thunderclap. Why do you not say that if I had never associated with such a man as Warby, I should never have been implicated in the first place?"

"I am not here to assess the wisdom of your actions; you are the best judge of them, not me," Philip retorted, "Mr. Brandon has offered me hospitality for tonight. I have a spare horse with me. I will be ready as soon as the sun is up."

"Is that all you have to say, dear cousin! No word of congratulation, no expression of joy that an innocent man is to be set free?" Richard mocked.

"Naturally I am glad," Philip replied pleasantly. "Do you not want to know news of your family?"

"Well?" said Richard, eyebrows raised.

"Your father is in good health, though I fancy he has aged somewhat during the two years that you have been here. Your mother——" he hesitated. "The sentence was a great shock to her; she was ill for some time. Physically, she is in excellent health, now, but her mind has become strange; she imagines that you are a boy again, away at school, and will be coming home for the holidays. This is a great anxiety to your father, especially as the physicians can do nothing for her."

Richard said nothing. Some pious expression of regret was expected of him, no doubt, he thought; he had none to make. His mind was full of the glorious possibilities of freedom, the anticipation of returning to Roxton Park in triumph.

"Free!" he said, finally, on a long breath, as though

only by saying the word over and over could he make it the truth. "God, you cannot know what this means! Easy for you who have lived soft! Look!" he thrust calloused, work-hardened hands towards his cousin. "What do you know of rough living? I have talked to men who helped build the road over those mountains! Some of their companions died from a dozen causes, and no one cared. This is a cruel country for those of us who were shipped out in the stinking Hells of convict ships."

"That is all behind you now," Philip said quietly; he felt it to be a failure within himself that he did not feel great affection for his cousin, and strove to right the balance by redoubling his efforts to be kind.

Richard threw back his head and laughed.

"Ah yes! Tonight I shall celebrate. And you will dine with the Lord of the Manor and his daughter!" he jeered.

"Miss Brandon is delighted that you are to be free. It seems she has succumbed to your charms!" Philip said lightly.

Richard glanced at him sharply.

"Why not?" he said arrogantly. "I am not like the rough men she is used to meeting in *this* place!"

"I think she is fond of you."

"So? What is that to me? I shall leave here, and never set eyes on this country again, thank God!" Richard retorted.

Philip replied that he would see him in the morning; Richard's eyes followed him thoughtfully, as he walked back to the house. He picked up his tools and began to walk back to the outbuildings, where he shared a hut with three other men. He was halfway there, when Taroola came towards him, walking more quickly than usual, joy in her eyes, and her light step, her long hair stirring in the breeze. Richard stood still, waiting for her. Comely enough, he thought, feeling his pulses stir; a good-looking young woman who made no secret, when they were together, of her feelings for him, which amused him. She was not coy; no downcast eyes, fluttering little phrases and sighs. Bold some would have called her, he thought; not that her behaviour was ever immodest, a fact he often regretted.

"Richard!" she cried softly. "So you are to be free! For that, I am so happy! But you will be gone from here and I do not know what I shall do. Would that I could go with you!"

He looked at the lovely, intelligent face, with its wide mouth. She was almost as tall as he was, and she rode a horse beautifully; he did not love her, though he had wanted her, many times; but there were few opportunities to be alone and certainly never a chance to possess her as he desired; her father kept too vigilant a watch; and when he died, she would be a rich woman, Richard reflected.

"I will come back for you, one day!" he promised lightly.

She put a hand gently on his arm.

"Do you mean that, Richard?"

"I swear it," he said solemnly. "I shall come as a free man next time, not a convict! But I must go home to England; my father is an old man, and my mother is ill. When I come back we shall be wed," he promised rashly, certain that he would never be called upon to honour such a promise.

She looked wistful.

"Do not stay away too long, Richard," she begged him. "You may forget me, once you have returned to England!"

He pulled off the small gold signet ring he wore, and handed it to her. "Keep that until I come back," he told her. "I could not stay long from you!"

She closed the fingers of her hand tightly over the ring; her face had none of the proud aloofness that Philip had seen, and her lips trembled.

"The days will seem long, until then," she said. "I

will be up at sunrise," she added, "to see you go; it is only for a little while, dearest Richard."

He smiled, and kissed her, in the shelter of the buildings. No one saw them; she turned back to look at him, once, standing there like a young god, his pale hair shining in the sun.

James Brandon was eager to hear about England; Taroola sat silent at the dinner-table, withdrawn and making only as much speech as politeness demanded. Philip felt vaguely sorry for her; her father was gentle, as though he understood the reason for her distress.

"Will you ever return to England?" Philip asked.

"I think not," James said.

"Have you no relations there?"

"Yes." James' voice indicated clearly that he had no desire to answer further questions. "In Kent. I have not seen them for many years."

But you came of good stock, Philip thought shrewdly. The books, the table appointments, the obvious culture and education. Why did you leave England, I wonder.

After the meal was over and Taroola had left them, James fetched out the chess board, and the box of ivory pieces.

"I seldom have the chance to play," he said, "You play, Mr. York? Good." Abruptly, he added:

"So you do not hold it against me that I shall be pleased to see the departure of your cousin?"

"No," said Philip.

"Taroola will forget him. But I am not easy about her. She is a woman of spirit, with a mind of her own. We had a governess for her when we first came here, but since she was ten years old, I have educated her myself. She has few friends; the manager's wife; Annie who has looked after her since she was a child. That is all. She may well be still unmarried when I die. In that case, she might wish to return to England. Mr. York, you are a man I can trust. If my daughter comes to England, she will know no one."

"But you have relatives!" Philip said.

"Yes." The voice was curt. "I have not seen them for many years. They hold me responsible for the death of Taroola's mother, by bringing her out here, to this country, against their wishes. It is an old, sad story of family quarrels, Mr. York; I have neither the time nor the strength to go back over old ground, now. Mary *wanted* to come with me; we were very happy. Well," he added, suddenly, "do I have your permission to tell my daughter that she may contact you, if ever she is in England, and needs help or advice?"

"Certainly," Philip said calmly.

"Thank you," James Brandon said simply. "I am grateful to you."

Philip was both astonished and intrigued; he gave his promise with every intention of honouring it, though doubting that he would ever be called upon to do so.

They talked about other things; Philip heard of James' pride in Taroola, his belief that Australia had a great future, his liking for the vast countryside, so different from the cosy greenness of England; he talked of the fascinating animals and birds, the strange ways of the aborigines, and the men who came looking for land; the harshness, the droughts, the setbacks, the loneliness. Philip listened, enthralled, and it was late when James finally bade him good night. He went to bed, but not to sleep; he tossed restlessly, and fell into doze, roused suddenly by a faint sound.

He got out of bed, and went to the door of his room; he was not entirely familiar with his surroundings, but he could hear James Brandon's heavy breathing, the call of a nightbird in the trees outside; and then, away to his left, a sound he recognized: Richard's soft laugh.

Reluctantly, he turned in the direction of the sound; it was also the direction of Taroola's room, he realized. He moved softly, and heard her voice, quick and breathless, though he could not catch the words, and then that soft laugh of Richard's again.

Philip went silently back to his room, with a feeling of sick disgust; he knew Richard's way, but he had not thought that Taroola held herself so cheaply.

Richard had come to her window; he would never have been so incautious, fearing discovery by her father, but for the fact that he had over-celebrated his freedom, and was slightly tipsy.

Taroola heard him; she jumped from bed, pulled a shawl around her shoulders, and ran to the window; he seized her hands, and began to kiss her face passionately.

"Let me come in!" he whispered.

"No, Richard! Dearest—*no!* My father would kill you if he found you here! And it is not right. One day we shall be married, and then—" she broke off; she had never used the word 'married' before.

Richard laughed, pulling her close, feeling the softness of her flesh, the thrust of her breasts, against him. Little prude, he thought scornfully; just like all the other pretty girls, after all—prime and coy, afraid of yielding up their precious virtue. He thought of a woman he had once tumbled, the wife of a Sydney store-owner for whom he had worked. She had been fat and coarse, but he remembered her eagerness to please him, her enjoyment of the way in which he had taken her. Women had always fallen into his hands like ripe peaches from a sunny wall, he thought, knowing the fierceness of his urgency to possess Taroola; it was too long since he had been with a woman.

"Your father is asleep!" he whispered, against her cheek. "Let me come in! I will be gentle." He laughed again, pulling her closer.

Scarlet-cheeked, she pulled free, and shook her head vehemently; thwarted, angry, he let her go. She could not see the fury in his eyes, as he stumbled away. Soon,

he would be back in England, there were plenty of
women there, ready to share his bed. How credulously
she had swallowed his tale about coming back! He had
given her his ring; she had refused to give herself to
him. She would never have the chance again.

Taroola climbed back into bed, trembling; she was
angry with herself because she knew she had wanted
him. She shook back her hair, her face proud and angry; it would have been right, because she loved him;
wrong, because they were not yet married. And she
was lost between those two extremes, confused, unhappy, in spite of the ring that she had hidden under
her pillow.

She was up before sunrise; preparing and packing
food; she brought the horses to the front of the house
herself. Her father was still sleeping, worn out by the
unaccustomed late night, and Philip curtly refused the
breakfast she offered him.

She looked at him in surprise; she disliked him, not
only because she knew he did not like Richard, but because she considered him arrogant and self-righteous.
She thought he looked at her even more coldly this
morning, and, as a result, she was cool towards him.

The morning was fresh and clear, untouched and
beautiful, in the sunrise; the noise of the river stepping
over boulders as it looped around the green hillock,
was like faery laughter; the bush was full of the sounds
of morning, from the birds and animals who had been
there long before men came, with their wives and
families and possessions, pushing their way westwards
in search of freedom, riches, adventure. I could almost
have loved this country, Philip thought, under different
circumstances.

James awoke in time to say good-bye to Philip.

"I am sorry you could not stay awhile," he said. His
eyes flicked over Richard, without liking, but he wished
him, civilly enough, a pleasant journey home. Richard

went from the room without replying; the old man lay back against his pillows, looking tired and drawn, as though he did not want to face the day.

"I shall not see England again," he said, to Philip, "though you may see Australia once more. If you come back, you will always be welcome here. I wish you a safe journey home, Philip York."

Taroola and Richard were talking by the fence when Philip left the house; Taroola's head was bent, and Richard was holding her hand; but at the sight of Philip, she drew back, and lifted her head, her smile cool for him.

"I trust you will have a good journey, Mr. York," she said formally.

He inclined his head; though she was tall, she barely reached his shoulder. He looked down into her beautiful dark-blue eyes that had the steely look of the English Channel on a winter day about them, and thought bitterly that all women were cheats and liars.

He and Richard mounted their horses; silently, side by side, they rode away. Richard turned frequently to wave, but not until they were almost out of sight did Philip turn for a last look at Taroola; the buildings lay sprawled against the green hill, neatly fenced; beside the gate, stood a still figure, her reddish hair flowing down over her shoulders. He could not see her face clearly, but he knew that she was crying, and he felt a moment's reluctant pity for her. She was weak and he had thought her strong; she was Richard's mistress, and he would not have believed she was a woman to give herself lightly; but he could understand her unhappiness, and the feeling of desolation within her.

CHAPTER TWO

Richard was impatient to reach Sydney, which Philip could well understand; he talked of his return to England, with all his old arrogance and boastfulness.

"Your father needs you at Roxton," Philip told him. "There is a great deal to do, and he too old to manage the affairs of the estate as he once did."

"I cannot bury myself at Roxton," Richard retorted impatiently.

Philip looked at him in surprise.

"What will you do, then?"

Richard shrugged and made no reply, his light eyes wary.

"Your father needs you—" Philip began; but Richard cut him short.

"*I* do not need a lecture, Cousin Philip!" he retorted curtly. "How soon do you suppose it will be before we can sail?"

Philip shook his head; Richard was insistent that they should sail for England as soon as there was accommodation on a ship leaving the port. Philip was naturally anxious to return, on his own account, and knew he would be glad to be home, with Richard safely restored to his parents. He understood Richard's wish to be rid of the country to which he had come, in chains, as a convict. He spoke of it, vehemently, to Philip.

"Clean linen and soft beds and good food! You have never been without them, Cousin! Nor have you travelled in the holds of ships where the air comes as hot as from an oven, and they put out all lights below decks, in order to save the oil. Aye, it is dark, there, with no room to move, the smell of sweating bodies, and the curses and crying of those who will be dead before morning. Food enough to keep you alive, if your stomach can hold it! For the stench of sickness when the seas are rough and scent of men dying are loathsome, but far worse than all the nausea in one's stomach, is the feeling of being trapped, battened down, knowing *nothing!* We do not know what storms or reefs or rocks we encounter, or what is happening up there on deck where the air is sweet and clean and the wind runs free!"

It was an impassioned speech that touched Philip deeply; he saw the bitterness and anger in his cousin's face, and tried to imagine himself in the hold of a convict ship. He shivered, and said quietly:

"Rest assured that I shall arrange for our departure from Sydney, with all possible speed. At least you will travel home in comfort, though I cannot answer for the mood of the sea!"

Richard smiled; satisfaction spread through him in a glow of well-being. It was all as he had painted it to his cousin, and the memory of it left a bad taste in his mouth. Well, it was all done now. He would be back in England before summer, and would spend a while at Roxton to please his father; after that, his time and his life would belong only to him.

He thought of the previous night, when Taroola had refused him gently, but with firmness. He had given her the ring as a gesture, one of his few generous acts, because she had been kind to him; he had wanted her, often, during the long, hot days on the sheep station, but her father had been vigilant for his daughter's honour. England, Richard reflected, was full of women as lovely, as desirable—and a good deal more accessible.

They were forced to stay several days in Sydney, which irked Richard considerably; he questioned his cousin closely about Matthew Warby's confession, but Philip could tell him little, beyond expressing the opinion that it was natural for a dying man to want to rid his soul of all evil he had done to others.

"And was my father pleased?" Richard asked.

"Have I not told you so?" Philip answered, surprised. "Only his age and your mother's state of mind prevented him from coming himself to bring you the good news and take you home; that is why he asked me to do so."

"Well, you have no ties, dear Cousin!" Richard mocked gaily. "No wife, nor child, nor parents to detain you in England!"

Nor any kin save for Sir Thomas, who was his mother's brother, Philip reflected bitterly. He thought of Taroola, who was beautiful in a way that few women were; the proud lift of her head, the lovely way she walked, her hair the colour of polished horse chestnuts, her eyes as deeply and intensely blue as the flowers that grew amongst the Scottish heather; her skin was like buttermilk, her features clear cut. Her mother must have been a great beauty, he thought absently; Taroola would not pass unnoticed anywhere. It could not be easy for her father to be vigilant; especially in a wild country where women were few and men were greedy . . . he thought of Richard's soft laugh, and felt sudden, appalling hatred; the moment passed over him, like a storm, and he was calm again.

Nearly a week after they had left Taroola, Philip and his cousin sailed from Sydney Harbour in the *Princess Caroline*. The great ship took the sea beautifully, her sails swelling in the wind; she breasted the waves as though she spoke with calm assurance for the safety of passengers and crew on the long voyage.

Richard stood on deck, watching the Australian coastline grow smaller, and fade into the distance; he drew huge lungfuls of fresh, salt air. He was well-pleased with life. The money that his father had sent by Philip had purchased him a new outfit of clothes, the best that Sydney had to offer, and he contemplated the voyage with lazy pleasure.

The voyage seemed long to Philip; Richard went ashore whenever they touched port, making it clear that he had no wish for his cousin's company. On most occasions he came back unsteady on his feet, full of drink. Philip knew better than to caution him as to his behaviour; he would be mocked for being a prig. He had done what he had promised to do; once they were back at Roxton Park, all responsibility towards his cousin was ended.

It was, on the whole, an uneventful voyage; they arrived back in England on a soft summer day, when the meadows were hazed with heat, and the cuckoo called sleepily from the coolness of green woods. The Somerset countryside was at its most beautiful when Richard and Philip drove through the high, iron gates of Roxton Park.

The house was larger and more splendid than Russington Towers, Philip's home, a few miles away; their lands adjoined, divided by a wide, shallow stream.

Roxton was an old house of considerable age, built of grey stone, with deep-set mullioned windows, and a great round tower. The wings that had been added to the house had become part of it, with the passing of the years, blending into a harmonious whole; thick creeper made a curtain around the heavy oak door; behind the house were lawns that rose, smooth as satin and the colour of emeralds, to thick beechwoods that made a picturesque backcloth.

On the top of each tall pillar that supported the wrought-iron gates was a carved stone horse, mane and tail flying as though it had been stilled in a gallop; Philip had always admired the stone beauty of the horses, and thought it a pity that no one had ever known the name of the sculptor.

The lodge-keeper's wife and children were waiting,

bright-eyed and curious, to bob and curtsy; Richard ac-
knowledged them with charm and an air of benevolent
kindness, which was not difficult for he was in a good
mood. He had never expected to see Roxton again;
certainly he had never dreamed he would return in
style, as he was today, in the coach decorated with his
father's coat of arms. The sun was shining, and the
world was a splendid place; the convict ship, Australia,
the camp, the hard work on the station, were fragments
of a nightmare. Taroola, the woman, he remembered
scarcely at all; thoughts of the future filled his whole
horizon.

The Baronet, Sir Thomas, came out to meet his son,
in the summer sunshine. Richard reflected, fleetingly,
that his father was more bent, more white about the
temples, that was all; he looked at the tall, stooping
man with the heavy dewlaps, and the mournful, span-
iel-eyes, and thought that it would be easy, as it always
had been, to get his own way with him.

Behind her husband came Lady Eleanor, giving a
small whimper of delight when she saw her son. Her
eyes had a vague look about them; an untidy loop of
grey hair hung down one side of her face, though she
was immaculately dressed and wearing a great deal of
jewellery.

"Dearest Richard!" she cried joyfully. "My dearest
child, home again for the school holidays! I thought
this last term would never end!"

There was a moment's embarrassed silence, before
Richard kissed his mother as though there was nothing
wrong, and said lightly to his father:

"Well, I am home, as you see, and a better voyage
back than going out, to be sure."

Philip saw the brightness of his Uncle's eyes, the way
his hands shook; but his voice was calm, as he said:

"Welcome home. We have a great deal to talk about,
you and I."

Philip saw an odd look in Richard's eyes, for a moment; curiosity, uncertainty, he could not say what it was.

"But first we must have tea!" Lady Eleanor cried, like a child afraid it will be overlooked.

Sir Thomas turned to his nephew; Philip thought, startled, that he had never seen him look so old or so tired. Surely he was glad to have his son safe home again? At all events, he seemed to be, judging by his welcome. But he looked like a man who carried a great burden of sorrow.

"Thank you, Philip," he said, with an effort. "I am grateful for what you have done to bring Richard home to me; that you well know. It is a debt that I shall be glad to repay if ever the need arises. And now, will you eat with us? You must be tired."

"It is kind of you sir," Philip said, "but I am anxious to be home, at Russington, if you will spare me your coachman and carriage for the journey. I will ride over and call upon you tomorrow; this is a reunion at which I can only be an interloper!"

"Oh, charmingly said, Philip!" Richard mocked lightly. His father's look rested thoughtfully upon him, and he was silent. Philip had the feeling that it would be less easy in the future for Richard to indulge himself as he had done in the past, without thought for his parents.

"Dear Philip, you are most welcome!" Lady Eleanor said gaily. "It is such a joy to have my baby home safe from school. It has been a *very* long time, you know, and they have told me I must be patient, but I have missed him . . . he is such a dear child, so full of life. . . ."

"And now you have him back," Philip said gently.

His uncle protested that he would not be an interloper if he desired to stay; Richard looked sulky as though annoyed that the limelight had been deflected from him, and Philip insisted courteously that he would like to return to Russington as soon as possible; he made his farewells and the carriage took him back down the drive, out through the gates, and along the road. He thought how beautiful it was, the more so after long absence; dog roses tangled in the hedges, a chorus of sleepy bird song, hum of bees in the clover, no breeze to bend the long grasses where the cattle lay in what tree-shade they could find; he looked at the dark, cool beechwoods that stretched out from Roxton to narrow into a thin coppice behind Russington; he had a sudden vision of Taroola walking there, her hair flowing free, her eyes filled with joy as they had been when he brought his news of Richard's pardon; and he was angry that she should nudge the hem of his thoughts like a small, timid ghost, when he wanted only to forget her.

The gates of Russington were not so tall or so splendid as those of Roxton; no stone horses galloped in frozen immobility on the high stone pillars; but the house, though smaller, was charming, with the same deep-set windows and tall chimneys, the same smooth lawns and thick, dark privet and box carved into the shapes of birds.

He knew very well who would come to greet him first of all: Emmy Gaunt, who had come to Russington with his mother, when she had married his father, and had looked after him since he was a baby. She ignored the outraged manservant who had opened the door as the carriage approached; she ran past him, and out to Philip, hobbling a little even though the warmth of the summer sun was kind to her rheumaticky joints, the strings of her cap flying, her starched apron rustling importantly. She had a face as round and smooth as a ripe apple, grey hair, the shrewdest eyes and kindest smile in the world.

"Welcome home, Master Philip!" she said breathlessly, using the old, childhood name. "Sir, it's good to see you! Sir Thomas sent over yesterday to say you were coming, and I couldn't believe it, not after all this time, and a terrible voyage, all that way across the world and back . . . !"

"It wasn't very terrible, Nanny!" He laughed, using the old nickname that she liked. "It's good to be home, though."

She nodded, her mouth suddenly buttoned up with disapproval; she had the privilege of speaking her mind to him that no one else in his household enjoyed; and she had not wanted him to go to Australia to bring home the cousin whom she declared richly deserved his sentence; even though she had grudgingly conceded that there was no one else to send. Even when he had been found innocent, her final word on the subject had been to the effect that if Sir Thomas and Lady Eleanor had not made such a fool of the boy, and given into his every whim, then he would never have got himself into such trouble in the first place.

Philip went into the house, acknowledging the greetings of the servants, listening absently to Nanny's chatter, retailing him all the local gossip. He washed and changed into clean linen, and took his tea in the long drawing-room where his mother had played the spinet on summer evenings such as this; he thought how peaceful the house seemed, after the long weeks at sea, with all his anxieties over Richard's behaviour; and yet he was conscious of a loneliness such as he had never experienced before.

He was tired, he told himself; tomorrow, the business of the estate would occupy him again. He would ride round with his bailiff, visit every one of his tenants and farmers; he had tried to manage the affairs of the land that was his as he knew his father would have wished.

Summer, that year, was gracious; the long days heavy with warmth, the nights bland as cream. Even with October, and the harvest gathered in, and beech-woods lit with summer's fires, there was still a mildness

in the air, a lazy mellowness that lay with dreamy
gentleness over all the countryside.

Philip, who had been away too long for his liking,
found that his days soon fell again into their accepted
pattern; he was a conscientious squire, his farms, his
cottages, the best-kept in the County; his land well
tilled, his people well cared-for. He knew of the discontent, the riots, the unrest, in other country areas, because of the poverty that had come to the countryside.
It was whispered that there would soon be huge en-
gines pulling carriages along an iron road carved
through the lush countryside; Philip thought that it was
not such a fantastic rumour as it had once seemed,
though the men who gathered in the bar of 'The Tank-
ard' of an evening laughed the idea to scorn; but new
factories were being built, especially in the north, and it
was said that there were towns over which a pall of
smoke hung like a funeral cloth, come summer, come
winter, and a man couldn't taste clean air any more,
there was poison in his lungs with every breath he took.
But there was money to be had in the big industrial
towns, and a good living; the countryside was in bad
way, there wasn't enough work, the houses and farms
were neglected unless you were lucky and had a good
squire. No one thought a great deal about the grand-
sounding word 'progress' in the sleepy county where
Russington and Roxton stood almost side by side; true,
Sir Thomas Roxton's tenants had a harder time of it
than Squire York's; for old Sir Thomas had let his
farms and cottages become neglected, and the women
gossiped about the ways of men and the world, as they
sat at their lace pillows, busy with the bobbins, looking
up from their doorways to see the handsome young
man who rode by on horseback, and telling themselves
it was a great shame that Squire York had no wife
beside him. . . .

So summer melted into autumn, and Richard was
still at Roxton Park, in spite of the boasts to himself

that London would soon see him again. There was a change at Roxton, Philip had noticed; Sir Thomas seemed older and more careworn, not rejuvenated by the return of the son who was to have taken the burden of managing a vast estate from his shoulders. Richard seemed peevish as a child, discontented, irritable, given to outbursts of anger, and took no interest in the estate; he seemed almost held there against his will, Philip reflected; probably Sir Thomas had reminded him of his duties and the good fortune that Matthew Warby's conscience had brought him; certainly, only Eleanor Roxton seemed happy; for, although her mind was in no way restored to its former health by her son's return, she was delighted to have him at home.

The nearest town to both Roxton Park and Russington Towers was Quinton St. John; a sizeable country town with good shops, a cattle market, a Town Hall, and a very old Church, with a large rectory beside it.

The houses near the Church were the finest in the town. In Abbott's Close, they were grouped around a small green park, with high railings, and a gate to which only the residents had a key; the houses were large, and it was a mark of one's social standing to live in one of them. In this elegant backwater, the residents considered themselves far above the common herd. They were mainly professional people, and counted themselves only one step removed from the gentry who inhabited such places as Roxton Park.

Number Three Abbott's Close had been empty for some time, until one day there was a great deal of activity, with furniture arriving, women coming to clean, staff engaged to look after the new tenant, who was expected within a few days. Gossip had it that she was a lady, recently widowed and well-to-do, with a young son.

She came on an autumn afternoon, when the sun was shining and a small breeze mischievously filched the last leaves from the trees to send them scurrying along gutters, with a mouse-like pattering. She was a small woman, quietly but expensively dressed in plain dark clothes. She looked sober and well-bred, so that the tenants who saw her arrival nodded approvingly and gave sighs of relief. Behind her came a nursemaid, a tall, gaunt young woman with sandy hair, who led a little fair-haired boy of about three by the hand.

The door closed behind the three people; Mrs. Able, the housekeeper, presented the cook and the two maids to Mrs. Caldecott. Esther Caldecott greeted them briefly, and stated that she would like tea served in half-an-hour in the drawing-room; then she went up to the nursery. Not until she saw Sebastian safely installed did she go to her own rooms. She told the boy he should come downstairs and she would read to him for an hour after tea; he was a pretty child, but spoilt, with a petulant mouth; given to harassing his nursemaids— none of whom ever stayed long—by screaming furiously and kicking them if he was thwarted in any way.

In her own rooms, Esther looked around thoughtfully, and nodded, with great satisfaction; it would do very well, she thought. The setting was exactly what she wanted.

She removed her outdoor clothes, and surveyed herself in the heavy mirror, framed in gilt cupids, between red velvet drapes; she smoothed her hands over her hair, down her body to her thighs, with an air of assessment.

Most people would have called her plain. She was quite slightly built, and looked frail. Her smooth hair was the colour of pale honey. Her face was fair-skinned and rather non-descript, but she had brilliant, light green eyes which were startling and unusual. They were large, seeming to dominate her face, and had a curious magnetism that people found compelling. With her soft voice and quiet demeanour, and enormous, brilliant eyes, she compelled attention.

They were eyes that could enchant, command, be

cold, hold secrets, flash fire. They were never warm and teasing; and combined with her smallness, her softness and quietness, they gave her the feline quality of a cat.

The maid brought a pitcher of water; Esther washed, and then went down a shallow, curving flight of stairs to take tea alone in the drawing-room overlooking the park, and consider her next move. She had never been to Quinton St. John before; she had rented the house for a year, which was a great extravagance, but she needed time, she reminded herself. The business upon which she had come would take time to execute, and she would have to be patient. She smiled to herself, well content with life; tomorrow, she would hire a carriage, and drive around the town, with Sebastian.

So, the following afternoon, a hired coach came to the door of Number Three, and Esther set out, with her son, having told the child's nurse that she need not accompany them, but that was no reason for idleness, and she would make herself useful indoors, for there was much to be done; a sentence delivered in the silk-soft voice that had steely undertones.

The town was larger than she had imagined; it was market day, and there was more traffic than usual. Sebastian was over-excited, climbing up and down on the seat of the coach; when the tour of the town was ended, she told the driver that she would like to drive out into the countryside, which, she had heard, was very pretty. Wasn't Roxton Park only a few miles away?

"To be sure it is," he said, in his soft, broad West Country voice; so they left the town, and Sebastian cried because the country lanes were dull, and the coach bumped and jerked over the ruts, making him feel sick.

They rounded a bend, and the coachman slowed the horses obediently; Esther took a long look from the window, feeling a small shiver of excitement run through her. There it was! She had never seen it before, and had not imagined it was so big. She looked with shining eyes at the carved horses, the high gates, at the great, grey bulk of the house itself, crouched below the beechwoods like a lion sleeping in the sun. How beautiful it was! She sighed and leant back against the seat, drawing a long, deep breath of immense satisfaction; it was so much grander than she had expected.

Autumn became winter almost overnight; the wind had an edge as sharp as broken glass and the skies were surly. In spite of her own counsel of patience, Esther found that time dragged. She entertained a little, behaving with a decorum and air of well-bred reserve that pleased her neighbours. She was always ready to listen to their talk of the town and the people in it; inevitably she heard the startling story of how Sir Thomas Roxton's only son had been wrongly accused of robbery and violence and transported to Australia, to return in triumph when his innocence was proved; she looked wide-eyed and impressed and made appropriate comments about justice . . . of herself she said little, maintaining a silence about her affairs that gave rise to wild speculation behind her back. She had hinted, delicately, that her husband had been a wealthy man and she had been his ward, since the death of her parents; but with only those few meagre crumbs would she satisfy their curiosity.

The opportunity will come, she told herself; she listened and watched and talked when it suited her, gathering her information carefully; she heard that old Sir Thomas was failing, that his son was supposed to be managing his affairs and a poor show he seemed to be making of it; and on a dour November afternoon she saw the coach with the Roxton coat of arms parked near a haberdasher's shop. Richard was just disappearing into an office across the street.

Esther went into the haberdasher's, lingering near

the door, pretending to be unable to decide between
the merits of the ribbons and laces displayed, her eyes
on the horses impatiently pawing the ground. From
where she stood she had an excellent vantage point;
when she saw Richard emerge from the offices, she said
charmingly to the hovering assistant that she simply
could not make up her mind, and would return another
day.

She timed it neatly; ignoring her own coach, parked
near Richard's, she began to cross the road, head bent.
As she almost walked into him, he put out an impatient
hand to steady her, and exclaimed angrily—until she
lifted her head, and he saw the pale face, between its
bands of light, lustreless hair, the brilliant green eyes.

His own face looked suddenly startled and faintly
uneasy.

"Why, *Richard!*" she said softly; a farm cart passed
close to them, the driver calling them to get out of the
way, and Richard hastily steered her across the road,
glowering. He was in a foul temper; his father's health
had kept him prisoner at Roxton, and he had scarcely
seen London—and now, *she* was here, the last person
he had expected or wanted to see.

"What brings you here?" he demanded, astounded.

"A poor greeting after such an absence!" she
reproved gently. "I have been waiting a long time to
see you, Richard!"

"We have nothing to say to one another!" he retorted.

"You are wrong." Her voice was as gentle as a summer day. "We have much to say to one another."

"Everything was said between us long ago."

She shook her head and smiled at him; her hand lay
on his arm for an instant in what looked like a pretty,
timid gesture; but he felt the strength in her fingers, the
determination in that brief grip.

"Do you not want to see your son, Richard?" she
asked; and when he said nothing, she added:

"Well? Will you let me dismiss my coach, and have your coachman take us where I am living?"

"I am in a great hurry," he replied.

"It would be wiser," she said softly, "if you came!"

He laughed shortly.

"And if I do not? What then? Will you threaten to disclose my indiscretions to your neighbours? Surely you realize the folly of such an act? For you will be considered nothing better than a whore! It is the privilege of young men, not young women, to sow their wild oats."

"I am not a whore, Richard. No man ever took me but you." Her eyes blazed. "You know it is so! And if you think I would use that fact as a bargaining point, then you misunderstand me! I have other, more important things to discuss!"

She smiled and he looked suddenly wary; it was a wide, knowing smile, that of someone who can afford to be patient.

"Very well!" he said irritably, "but I have precious little time to spare. Where are you living? With whom?"

"At Abbott's Close. Alone with my son and the servants. My husband, Mr. Caldecott, is dead." Her smile was very gentle.

"Caldecott? Your husband! No such person ever existed!" he sneered.

"You are right; but I have found him useful. It is equally useful to be his widow."

A few curious passers-by saw Richard help Mrs. Caldecott into his carriage, and give directions to the surprised driver; he sat, stiff and silent, beside her throughout the journey, trying to dismiss the faint feeling of uneasiness within him. How could she possibly harm HIM, he thought angrily! The idea was absurd; it was a trick, to insinuate herself into his life again, and one he would not tolerate.

He looked at her, admitting grudgingly that she still

had a certain physical attraction for him; he remembered how those great cat's eyes had shone, how her small, soft body had twined itself about him in an ecstasy of love-making, her arms around his neck, pulling his head down to hers. She looked as small and colourless as a snowflake, but she had shown a passion that had astonished and delighted him. He remembered the first time; a hayrick, soft, sweet-smelling; the summer afternoon had lengthened into evening, before she had let him go; there was the house to which she had taken him, near Norfolk; musty-smelling, shrouded with dust-sheets, shut up for months, she had told him—all except the one room in which she had lighted a fire and aired a bed. He remembered that she had come to him, her loosened hair falling below her waist, her naked limbs white in the firelight . . . in spite of all that had happened afterwards, he felt desire stir faintly but insistently within him; he thought he knew very well what she wanted of him. She would dismiss the servants, and then smile and hold out her arms. She wanted money for the child, and she would pay him for it in kind. If she thought he was rich, that he had plenty for the boy, then he would soon rid her mind of such a notion; he frowned, biting the tip of his thumb, thinking how strangely his father had behaved this morning, walking as though he was drunk, his face red, his hands sweating. God, he thought, with an ache of self-pity, that he should have come home to THIS!

Esther took him indoors, and ordered tea; there was a fire burning in the drawing-room, and she stood beside it, one hand on the mantelshelf, as she smiled at him. She looked small and defenceless.

"I will have Sebastian brought downstairs, after tea," she promised him.

"I have no desire to see him," he retorted.

"You are not married," she said softly. "Neither are you courting a suitable young woman, of gentle birth, as a possible mistress for Roxton and the provider of heirs for you!" Her voice mocked him. "And, certainly, you do not need to do so; you already have a son!"

He looked at her incredulously.

"Have you taken leave of your senses, Esther?"

"No." She shook her head, her voice so quiet he scarcely heard it. "I want us to be married, Richard. Then our son will live at Roxton and inherit it one day!"

He laughed; a hard sound, with more anger in it than amusement.

"I have no intention of marrying!"

"No?" She ran her hand the length of her body, in the long, smoothing gesture he remembered so well. "You like to take your sport where you please, Richard; but you are almost thirty. It is time you devoted yourself to more serious things. The estate is neglected, your father is ill, your mother has become strange in her mind; you need a wife."

"When I do," he retorted coldly, "I will choose her for myself. By Heaven, you have impudence!"

"Nevertheless, I think you will marry me. I have a document, Richard. One which you would very much like to have. I will give it to you on our wedding night."

When he left the house, some time later, his face looked pinched and white, his mouth was a thin line, his eyes hard, defeat lay upon him, sullen as a November fog. The coachman, seeing only Richard's anger and hearing his shouted instructions, drove fast through the murky evening, and said, afterwards, when he was talking over the day's events in the servants' hall, that it seemed almost as though Mr. Richard had had a kind of warning, a 'seeing' like the Scots have; a premonition of disaster, that's what it was. . . .

All the lights seemed to be on in the house; Richard scarcely noticed them. His one thought was to get to his father, who would know exactly what to do and how this situation must be dealt with. All his life his father had shielded him from whatever was unpleasant.

He tossed his cloak to the waiting servant and crossed the hall to his father's study; as he reached the door, his mother came out. Her eyes had their usual vague look, but she was frowning, as though she was vexed.

"Richard, dear, I am so glad that you have come home. Your father is asleep and I cannot rouse him, he will NOT awaken; it is so vexing, for there is something I want to tell him!"

Richard never discovered what it was his mother had been going to say to his father; he pushed past her, and went into the firelit study. His mother had lighted the candles in their sconces—his father preferred them to the new-fangled oil lamps. Sir Thomas was sitting in his high-backed chair, head and shoulders sprawled over the desk in front of him. Richard went forward and lifted him, his heart thundering loudly and painfully as he looked at the lolling head.

His father was dead; the one person in the world who could have helped him now, told him what to do, and found a way out of the maze in which he ran to and fro, looking for an exit, had left him to fend for himself.

Richard looked at the man in his arms, and felt a terrible storm of anger, a rage like that of his son, who screamed and lashed out when he was thwarted and could not have what he wanted.

CHAPTER THREE

Sir Thomas was buried in the family vault at Quinton St. John Parish Church, on a bitter November afternoon, the mourners standing under a funeral pall of rain that whispered down through the lifeless trees.

Richard hated every moment of it; the sour smell of decay in the newly-opened vault, the monotony of the preacher's voice, the rain, and the coldness that seemed to eat through his bones. He hated the silences, the hushed voices, the thin, scraping sound as the coffin was moved, and yearned passionately to be away from it all; he thought, suddenly, of the hot Australian sun. For a moment, temptation was a blinding, dazzling promise. Sell the house, land, farms, cottages; go back there, as a free man, to the sun, the warmth, the opportunities. Even to Taroola, which would be better than this . . . no one would find him there. . . .

Except Esther; she had promised him before he left the house in Abbott's Close the first time, that wherever he went she would seek him out.

He saw her standing in the Churchyard, in the shade of a yew, keeping her distance from the family mourners, almost completely hidden by the dark, hooded cloak she wore; but she lifted her face, for an instant, as her glance met his, and he knew, despairingly, that he had no choice. What would his father have done, he wondered desolately? Even he could not have foreseen this situation, nor could he have found a solution.

Esther had promised him the paper he wanted, on their wedding night. Very well then; he drew a deep breath. He would find some way of ridding himself of her, afterwards, when he had what he wanted.

" 'Tis a positively indecent haste!" said Nanny Gaunt grimly. "His father not dead two months, and him to be married almost at once!"

"Why, Nanny, what's that to do with it?" Philip said, with a touch of impatience. "He needs a wife, now, more than ever; he cannot entertain alone, nor run the place without a mistress; and his mother is more muddled in her mind than ever, since Sir Thomas died. A wife will steady him, comfort him and help him."

"I'm glad you think so, sir," she said, with a derisive sniff.

Philip looked at her, and his lips twitched; but he said firmly:

"She seems a quiet, sensible woman. I hope she will make him a good wife, and that they will be happy."

"There's something about her makes me unsettled in my mind," Nanny said. "A pity *you* wasn't thinking of marrying, sir. It's time past; you must have an heir."

"All in good time," Philip said, with a plain indication in his voice that the subject was closed; and Nanny, who knew exactly how far she could go, gathered up the linen she was mending for him, and looked out at the bleak landscape, the hills swaddled in folds of blue-white snow, the branches of trees heavy with the weight of it, the fields quilted with white. Winter had come like a bride; at night, she wore the stars like diamonds in her hair, and, by day, when the sun shone wanly from behind the clouds, she glittered with hoar frost as with jewels.

Master Philip should be married, she thought, plucking at her underlip; a man needed to find comfort in a woman's arms; he must have sons to make his old age happy. Not that Sir Thomas's son had ever done that; a spoiled little brat from the time he was born, Nanny thought scornfully. She shook her head, doubting that much good would come of his marriage to a woman about whom everyone knew so little, and whom she instinctively did not trust.

All winter, Philip had been restless; within him, there was a deep sense of discontent that dismayed him. He went to the library, and spread out the maps in front of him. Australia, the new country, discovered only a handful of years ago. He had heard stories of Captain Cook and the *Endeavour,* and the hardships they had endured, the impossibilities that they had made into possibilities. He thought of the hot sun, the strange chattering of birds and animals, unlike any oth-

ers he had ever seen, the huge trees; the road hewn out
of rugged mountains, the bearded men making camp
along the route to the West; and, as always, his
thoughts came to a halt with Taroola. He thought of
the last time he had seen her, standing by the gate of
her father's house, waving good-bye to Richard. He
could remember sharply how red her hair had looked
in the morning sun; angry, he turned away from his
thoughts. He would never see her again; he knew little
enough of her, though Richard, evidently, had known a
great deal. He had other things to think of, much to do,
ceaseless vigilance to keep for his own land and his
own people. The situation on the Roxton Estates was
uneasy; the men were sick of leaking roofs, damp cottages, weary of a landlord who never heard their com-
plaints. Some of the most venturesome young ones had
gone away to the cities in search of more money and a
better life; but many of them, especially the older ones,
born and bred in the country, shook their heads over
the idea of such an uprooting, even whilst they hated
the ties that bound them to Roxton Hall. On the Home
Farm, from which all the produce went to the Hall,
someone had fired a couple of hayricks and burnt down
a barn. The culprit had never been discovered; someone had also fired a small coppice, again on Roxton
land.

Philip had no such problems; he was well-liked and
respected. He gave fair exchange for what he received;
all his efforts to point out the wisdom of this policy to
his Cousin Richard failed lamentably. Richard had
snarled at him like a cornered animal; even his approaching wedding seemed to give him no great satisfaction which puzzled Philip. He had been invited to
meet Richard's future bride, and had found her
pleasant and agreeable. Truly a sensible woman, as he
had told Nanny; one who would bring Richard to an
awareness of his responsibilities. After all, Richard
could have become betrothed to some flighty little flib-

bertygibbet who would have run through what remained of the Roxton fortune, Philip thought; and Richard seemed bent on squandering the money his father had left—a sadly depleted sum at that, Philip suspected shrewdly—on his own pleasures. And all the while there was unrest because of Richard's neglect of the people who should have been his first concern, Richard had been making trips to London; where, it was rumoured, he lost heavily at the gaming tables, and took to bed, in his town house, any woman who captured his fancy. Philip wondered uneasily if rumours of this had filtered through to Mrs. Caldecott. He fancied so, for she had once said quietly to him:

"What Richard needs, Mr. York, is the steadying influence of someone to care for, someone at his side to counsel and help him, for I fancy he leaned heavily upon his father in such matters; he is very fond of my son, and, for my part, I am sure that I can help him in his daily work. The estate, from all I hear, is being neglected, and Richard seems to have no great interest in it; all that will be changed, I assure you."

The wedding was a quiet one, in February, when the first snowdrops, thickly clustered under the bare trees in Roxton Park, were showing their frail heads. The day was raw and cold, sunless, with snow flurries. Philip rode home from the wedding, remembering Richard's forced gaiety, the way he was drinking heavily, in sharp contrast to the gentle demeanour of his bride. He had a sense of foreboding. Esther Caldecott, now Lady Roxton, was not going to find it easy to keep Richard to the path she had mapped out for him.

Richard drank his way steadily through the evening; after their evening meal, alone together, Esther announced that she was tired, and would retire for the night; some time later he went up to the big room that had been prepared for them.

She sat in the big double bed, her long, fine hair

spread out against the pillows, a flush in her pale cheeks, her eyes as bright as jewels; she looked, if not beautiful, physically compelling in a way that roused him suddenly. Drink had dulled the sharpest edge of his anger against her, his bitterness for the marriage into which he had been trapped. She was, after all, his wife, with obligations that he intended she should fulfil. His surge of desire was purely for the small, smooth body beneath the bed linen, heightened by a memory of the old fires she had once lit within him.

She smiled, a curiously satisfied, amused smile; he stumbled to the bed and fell heavily across her, pinning her back against the pillows, his hands eager and urgent at the neck of her nightgown, his mouth seeking hers.

But she fought him off with all the supple strength and fury of a small tiger; she pulled a hand free, and he felt sudden, sharp pain in his cheek as her fingernails scored a thin line. The pain maddened him, her resistance inflamed a savage desire to inflict hurt upon her, as his hands tore at the thin fabric she wore, ripping it away; but she twisted, eel-like, from beneath him, and he instinctively reeled back from hands, claw-like, the nails seeking his face; so, with one final thrust, she was free, springing from the bed, holding the torn fabric to her throat, and looking at him with terrible hatred in her eyes.

"A fine welcome for your bridegroom, madam!" he snarled furiously, as he staggered, panting, to his feet, and faced her, the width of the bed between them. "So that is what you want, is it? A battle that will make the final surrender more sweet?"

"Surrender—to you?" she said contemptuously, venom in her voice. "Never, Richard! *Never!*"

He swayed unsteadily, holding to the bedpost.

"Once you came willingly!" he sneered. "You were like a woman with a thirst that could not be slaked."

"Once," she admitted bitterly. "You used me ill,

Richard. What of *your* appetites? You were a consider-
ate lover, at first; and as eager as I, until you became
contemptuous, not caring how you took me, and boasted of the other women who had shared your bed! I
have a son, remember, Richard," she added softly; and,
suddenly, with brutal candour:

"I want no more children of yours. This room, this
bed, is my own. I had not thought you would have
come like this, or I would have bolted the door against
you. If you come again, then I will rouse the whole
household and tell them that you have tried to murder
me because I will not yield to drunken rape!"

Her words sunk in slowly; all passion had gone, and
with it his brain cleared. He remembered the bargain
she had made, and said sullenly:

"The document you have promised me! Give it to
me!"

She smiled, head tilted to one side, eyes bright and
hard. *"And* the paper signed by your father! The most
damning evidence of all. I have that, too."

"Then give them to me, as you promised."

"No, Richard. Do you think me such a fool as to
give you the only weapon in my possession that will ensure I come to no harm? So long as *I* possess it, I am
safe. Once you have what you want, then you will seek,
by any means you can, to dispense with me."

She knew, he thought bitterly; she was shrewd
enough to be aware that he had no intention of letting
this ill-conceived marriage endure for longer than he
could possibly help; he had, as yet, formed no clear
ideas as to how he would rid Roxton of the unwanted
mistress he had put there. In his extreme moments, he
had thought, quite calmly, of ways in which to kill her
that would look as though she had suffered an accident.

Cheated, thwarted, he glared at her, moving around
the bed.

"Give me the paper!" he snarled softly.

She backed away from him; in spite of her cunning,

her contempt of him, she was momentarily frightened. She was strong, with a fine-boned, supple strength, but it would not match brute force, she knew; and she would have died before she let her fear of him show in her face.

"I do not have them with me!" she spat back. "Do you think I am twice a fool? They are carefully hidden until the day I may need them. Tear this place apart with your hands and you will not find where I have hidden them! I shall never tell you where they are, though you try to kill me!"

He knew she meant it; for the first time in his life, his exit was inescapably blocked, and he felt like a man clawing at a wall of glass, trying to find foothold. For a moment, murder glittered in his eyes, and she saw it, her heart beating fast; but the moment passed, the thin thread of reason did not snap within him. He struck her violently, and she fell across the bed; then he turned and went to his own room, lashed by a violent paroxysm of rage, tearing the covers from the bed, hammering at the walls with his fists until the very pain was a relief; then sobbing like a child, he flung himself across the disordered bed and finally slept. . . .

Esther rearranged the coverlet about her; there would be a bruise upon her face, by morning, where he had struck her, she thought, with satisfaction; the pain of it would be well worth bearing. The maid would notice the bruise, the torn nightgown, the empty space beside her; Richard would still be sleeping heavily, no doubt. She thought of the whispers below stairs, the sympathy for her, for Richard had a reputation, even amongst the servants, she knew.

She thought of Richard's despair, and laughed; he would never have married her, had he not seen the alternatives so clearly. It would not be the chains, the transport ship, the convict camp *this* time, as she had pointed out—he would be hanged. And she had reckoned on the one thing that Richard had, in common with all men and women, when faced with no alternative: that life is sweet, even in a loveless marriage. He would, eventually, find his own exits: London, his women there, the gaming tables. Well, she would put a stop to that, also, she thought. The Roxton Estates were to be preserved, made prosperous, as a fitting inheritance for her son. She saw no obstacles; Lady Roxton was harmless and old and not likely to live many more years. And, further along the road, an even more shining vision beckoned. . . .

She sighed, scarcely daring to think about it; but what if it could be? With Richard denounced, it would be easy—married to a man she had as yet met only briefly, but whom she wanted with the same passion that she had once shown for Richard. She compared the two of them; Richard, weak, silly as a girl, petulant, charming, with his fair good looks. And Philip York, dark, aloof, who had captured her imagination the moment she had met him. Her pulses quickened; he was not married, it was rumoured he had no time for a woman, but he liked and approved of her, she knew; a good beginning, she thought, contentedly; and when she was Richard's widow, what more natural than that she should turn to Philip? And what greater prize than the merging of both Roxton Hall and Russington? One day, she could be the richest, most powerful woman in the County. It was not such an impossible goal, if she was patient and clever and careful. . . .

She sighed, like a contented kitten; had it been Philip who had come to her, she thought, she would not have turned him away tonight.

It was almost a month before Philip and Richard came face to face, when they were both out riding, one fine spring morning, in the countryside beyond their estates. The snow had gone, the air had a gentle feel about it, the trees promised a great burgeoning of leaves in good time, and the sun was kind.

Philip, greeting his cousin, thought how haggard he looked; in point of fact, Richard was in a better mood than usual. He had returned from London the previous day having done well, for once, at the gaming tables. It had given him strength to ignore Esther's fury, laugh at her when she threatened to see him hanged. For once, she had been disconcerted, and he had wondered, then, about the documents; but he knew she did not lie when she said she had them, for she had shown him copies. Nevertheless, today he did not care; she could do as she pleased, he thought, greeting his cousin with more than usual civility.

Philip was thinking of Esther. There had been rumours of a disastrous wedding night, a drunken husband. Esther had asked him to dine, some days later, and had explained that the fading bruise on her cheek was the result of a fall, but she was a poor liar, he thought compassionately, and somehow she had not made the story convincing. Richard had not been present at the dinner, and she had apologized, saying he had unexpectedly been taken unwell. It was only later that she had admitted, tears in her eyes, that she did not know where he was. She had called at Russington on one or two occasions, to ask Philip's advice, and beg him to urge his cousin to attend more closely to the affairs of the estate. She had been so earnest, so concerned, he thought; and reflected, exasperated, that Richard did not deserve such a wife.

He broached the subject carefully:

"I have seen Jonathan Staker's cottage this morning, Richard; the next gale will send it flying like a witch on a broomstick! The place is unsafe, and the thatch rotten!"

"You spoil the morning!" Richard grumbled. "I have to endure enough of her nagging. God knows, without yours!"

"She nags to good purpose; she has your interests at heart. The state of your property is becoming a scandal, Richard, and you should be perturbed by the rumblings of discontent amongst your people!"

"Well?" Richard mocked, leaning negligently across his restive horse. "What am I expected to do, Cousin Philip? They are a lazy, shiftless lot!"

"That is not true," Philip said quietly, "as well you know. If they do not work as hard as they might, the fault is yours, for you cannot expect them to live worse than pigs in a sty and give of their best to you. They will repay you a hundredfold if you but give them a little consideration."

Richard laughed, though his eyes were angry.

"You match the Parson well for words! He should yield up his pulpit to you, on Sunday, for you might, certainly, keep the congregation awake as he cannot! But keep your sermons for those who want to hear them. Esther urges me to pour all my money into the land."

"A better place for it than the gaming tables," Philip observed.

Richard's eyes narrowed.

"That is my business. I have a cold wife, Philip, and must seek diversion elsewhere."

"Perhaps the remedy for her coldness lies in your hands, Richard."

"How little you know!" Richard sneered bitterly. "You have quite spoilt the day for me with your preachings!" he added pettishly. "There is no money! There, does that satisfy you? SHE will not believe that I am hard-pressed and in debt. You are a prosperous man, and fond of quoting that prosperity comes about by prudence; but let others live as they choose!"

He turned and galloped away, and Philip looked after the retreating figure; Richard was a little more than a month married, he thought grimly. He had never grown to manhood, and it was a poor outlook for his wife.

Spring became summer, and Philip recalled, with

surprise, that it was a year since he had come home to Russington; little had changed, at Russington. At Roxton, the situation seemed to be growing steadily worse; Richard, it was rumoured, quarrelled bitterly with his wife over his jaunts to London, and ignored his young stepson. Esther came to Philip often for advice and comfort, though she did not openly ask for nor revile Richard in any way. Philip found her loyalty to her husband immensely touching, and could not understand Nanny's continued dislike and distrust of Richard's wife.

The summer was hot; on an afternoon when the thick copper-coloured sky and warm, stale air promised a storm, one of the servants came to Philip and told him he had a visitor.

He was working on farm accounts, in his study; he put down his quill, rubbed a hand tiredly across his forehead, and said, puzzled:

"A visitor? Whom?"

"A young lady, sir. She says her name is Miss Brandon, and that you will know her."

Brandon? He frowned. Then he remembered; James Brandon's daughter, Taroola. Or, more conventionally, Anne Brandon. But it was not possible that she should be here, in England!

He got up hastily, and hurried past the astonished servant, into the hall.

She was sitting quietly, on an oak settle, her hands folded in her lap. Beside her lay the heavy cloak that she had obviously found too hot for comfort, and she wore a light dress of some pretty flowery material. The look she gave him was grave, uncertain, unsmiling; she had matured, in some way, he thought, and she was lovelier than ever, with her rich, mahogany-lustred hair coiled neatly instead of flowing loose, her eyes the same lovely dark blue in her clear-skinned face.

"Taroola!" he said, in astonishment, the old name coming instantly to him.

She smiled rather tiredly.

"It is a long time since I was called by that name!" she said wistfully.

It was a long time since he had seen her, he thought.

"Is your father well?" he asked.

She looked down at her hands for a moment, but when she lifted her face it was quite composed.

"He died only a short time after you left the station, Mr. York; a matter of weeks. He suffered a recurrent fever, as you know, and I think it weakened him. The final bout was fatal."

"I am sorry," he said quietly. "I knew little of your father, but I liked him. Will you take tea?"

She nodded, and stood up; escorting her to the drawing-room, he realized that he had forgotten how tall she was, how well she carried herself.

The drawing-room was cool, every window open to catch a capful of wind. He pulled the bell-rope and ordered tea for them both. Taroola sat on a small brocaded couch, looking cool, and he thought: she will not be aware of the heat, after living in Australia. He had never expected to see her again; astonishment was still uppermost that she should be sitting here, in his house.

"What brought you to England?" he asked, when the tea was set upon the table, and the doors closed behind the curious little maidservant.

She said calmly:

"I came to see your cousin, Mr. York." Her eyes met his challengingly. "When he left the station, he gave me this ring." She lifted her left hand and he saw the heavy gold signet ring that had been Richard's, gleaming on the third finger.

"He said that he would come back, Mr. York. I wrote to tell him of my father's death and I heard nothing from him. I wrote other letters; there was no word. I told myself that letters take many weeks to reach England—or Australia. I was sure that he would return, or that I would hear; in the meantime, it was difficult

for me to remain on the station. I did not want to sell
it!" He saw her angry, defeated look. "I had no option.
A woman cannot run a sheep station alone in the back-
woods of Australia, it seems!"

"Could you not have found someone to whom you
could have given your affection?" he asked. "Then you
would have had a husband to help you with the work
of the station."

Her chin tilted, in a gesture he suddenly remembered
well.

"No. I have given my affection elsewhere, as you
must know. Eventually, I had no choice but to sell; the
Authorities insisted that it was neither safe nor discreet
for me to do otherwise. So, I have come to England,
Mr. York; to see Richard."

It was simply said, but with immense dignity. He did
not feel pity for her, as he did for Esther, but rather a
tremendous admiration for her proud loneliness, her
single-mindedness.

"Have you been to Roxton Hall?" he asked quietly.

"No. I have taken rooms at the Inn, in the village."

"And you walked here—today, in this heat?"

"Why not? I am well used to the heat, and I do not
find two miles an overtiring walk!" she retorted.

"In England, young ladies do not walk country roads
unescorted, as a rule," he pointed out.

She shrugged indifferently.

"I cannot see what harm I shall come to; but I did
not go to Roxton, Mr. York, because when I made
enquiries in the village, I heard that Richard had been
married, these six months past. So I thought it more
prudent to call upon you, to know if these rumours are
true."

Rumours, he thought? Surely she knew that it must
be the truth, coming as it did, from the people who
lived almost in the shadow of the gates of Roxton. He
looked at the gleam of gold on her finger and remembered the sound of Richard's laughter in the night,

when he had been in Taroola's room.

"It is no rumour," he told her briefly. "Richard was married six months ago."

There was no sound in the room; the intense heat seemed to press against them like a weight too heavy to be borne.

"To whom?" she asked quietly, at last; her face was white.

"A young widow, with a son. Her name was Esther Caldecott. She is now Lady Roxton, of course."

"And they are happy?" she asked unexpectedly.

He met her glance with a hard one of his own.

"I do not think that Lady Roxton finds the path of matrimony easy. Richard does not change. His father died last autumn, and though he is now the owner of the estate, he has little liking for it."

"Why did he marry her?" Taroola demanded for-lornly.

"Presumably because he had a great affection for the lady," Philip retorted.

"Yet it seems to have diminished so soon!" she cried.

"I did not say that." He gestured to her to pour tea for them both and she did so gracefully, just as she had done all those months ago, on a hot afternoon, on an Australian sheep station.

"I said that the path of matrimony was not smooth for Richard's wife. He is not yet a man, with an awareness of a man's responsibilities."

He marvelled at the steadiness of her hands; her face was still very white. Philip guessed the truth; she had come, believing Richard would be unwed, that he would be at her journey's end with good reason to give her for his long silence.

Finally, she said:

"I thought that he must be ill, when I did not hear from him. At first, I believed that he would come back."

What a fool she was to have given herself to Richard, he thought! She was still infatuated with him, it seemed.

Nevertheless, he was concerned for her; confirmation of the truth had been a great shock to her, he realized. She had never considered that Richard would have given his ring without meaning to honour his promise.

"What will you do?" he asked gravely. "Will you seek out your father's and mother's relatives?"

"Indeed not," she said, curtly. "I have no wish to contact them, Mr. York. It is an old family quarrel."

Yes. He knew that; her father had told him so.

"Then what will you do?" he pressed. "You are alone, unprotected, you know no one."

"Do you try to persuade me, Mr. York, that it would be foolish to call at Roxton and make my presence known to your cousin?" she demanded sharply.

"No!" he retorted angrily. "I trust your own good sense will prevent such an occurrence. I am merely concerned for your immediate future."

"Then do not be." She stood up, almost matching him for tallness, her chin tilted in that defiant way that so infuriated him, her eyes bright, her mouth firm. "I am not entirely without means. My father has left me well provided for and I am able to take care of myself."

"How absurd!" he cried. "No woman can do that; she needs the protection of a man! You can stay here, for the time being, until one of your relatives can be contacted—much as you may dislike the idea, I fear you have no choice."

"I shall NOT go to my relatives, Mr. York; and I have no intention of disturbing Richard's marriage if *that* is what you fear!"

She was obstinate, stubborn, wilful, he thought angrily; let her go her way, if she was so determined. He glared down at her from his arrogant height; a sudden wind plucked at the curtains, and made the leaves on the trees shiver. He thought he heard a faint, far-off rumble, as though thunder walked the sky.

"There will be a storm," he said shortly. "At least, you will stay until it is over."

She shook her head; she was unhappy, exhausted, and close to tears. She had come to Russington, praying that rumour had lied. She was near to breaking point and had no intention of letting this proud, haughty cousin of Richard's discover that fact.

"I shall be at the Inn before the storm breaks," she assured him.

"That you will not." His ear caught a second rumble of thunder. "But if you are so set on it, then I will have the horses harnessed and escort you there."

"I have no wish that you should do so," she retorted.

"You will be soaked before you have gone half a mile!" he told her.

Misery made her more stubborn than she might have been, under happier circumstances. She had a desperate desire to be alone.

"I will go by myself," she told him.

"As you please, madam!" he said furiously. It was the first time she had ever seen him in a temper; controlled, as his fires would always be, she thought.

He went with her to the hall, and held her cloak for her; she adjusted the hood with suddenly unsteady fingers, knowing he would say nothing more to try to induce her to stay. In silence he walked to the gates with her, where she turned and gave him a brief, polite smile.

"Thank you for your hospitality, Mr. York. I doubt that we shall meet again."

She walked away, without looking back; he watched her, astonished. For the first time in his life a woman had out-matched him for sheer stubbornness, and anger shook him as a tree is shaken in a storm. She was a fool! he thought. Tomorrow, he would ride down to the Inn and tell her so. What could he do, though, for a woman who persistently rejected his help? She was of age; she would come to harm, he thought, perturbed and exasperated, an exceptionally good-looking young woman, of spirit and intelligence, and with means, alone in the world.

Tomorrow he would make her listen to him; when the first storm of grief had worn itself out, he thought, for he suspected she had taken the news of Richard's marriage very hard indeed.

The wind came again, as though trying to take the leaves in flight, and drops of rain fell coldly upon his upturned face. He called to the retreating figure, but she did not hear him; she walked, wrapped in her own grief like a second, invisible cloak, tears falling as she rounded a bend, and was lost from sight.

The rain came harder and heavier, the wind upon its heels; the first of the lightning flickered, as Philip strode indoors. Two miles, and she walked quickly; but the storm would be upon her, before she was much further. It served her right, he thought; a good soaking might cure her of much. He knew very well that he did not mean what he said to himself, that he was anxious about her.

The lightning flickered again, and the trees began to thrash about angrily, as though they feared the rape of the coming violence. The thunder was closer, full of anger. The servants scurried to close the windows and secure the shutters; they feared the lightning more than anything else. The rain began to plummet down so furiously that its voice was temporarily louder than the thunder. He had to go to her; he could not leave her alone in such a plight.

"It'll bring down the elm in the Churchyard," Nanny Gaunt told him, hurrying downstairs. " 'Tes rotten and should have come down long since. Why, Master Philip, where are you going . . . ?"

He was gone, leaving her open-mouthed, snatching

up his cloak, racing for the stables. He thought of the
elm, leaning over the Churchyard wall, on the road to
the village, struck by lightning, uprooted by the lashing
of the wind, crashing down upon her. . . .

Philip was soaked before he reached the stables; the
astonished groom had never saddled a horse so quickly
in his life. He might well have been pardoned for thinking his master mad, as Philip rode out into a curtain of
rain whose thick folds hid him from sight.

She would not have reached the Churchyard yet, he
reasoned; she would be sheltering somewhere along the
road. But where was shelter? The road ran for some
way between hedges, past a farm gate, under trees until
it came to the Churchyard. She would be quite unprotected from the elements.

Taroola had walked faster than he thought, and it
was difficult to see through the driving rain; and when
at last he came upon her, by the farm gate, he almost
passed her by, for she lay huddled in the road, where
she had fallen; her wet cloak was spread around her,
the thin material of her dress clung limply to her body.
He saw the blood on her cheek, and for one horrifying
moment believed her dead; but when he bent and lifted
her, she moaned, opening her eyes for a moment, before her head fell against his shoulder.

CHAPTER FOUR

He slid his arms beneath her body, but she was heavy,
in spite of her slenderness, and the wet, clinging cloak
did not help. He would never get her on to his horse,
he thought despairingly; but as he pulled her to her feet,
her eyes opened again, and she looked at him, a sad
lost look that filled him with compassion. The rain
streamed down her face, and her wet hair clung to her
cheeks.

"Can you help yourself at all?" he asked urgently, above the noise of the storm. "For, if you can, I can get you on to my horse, and get you back to shelter."

She nodded and roused herself with a tremendous effort, leaning against him, as he half walked her, half dragged her towards the horse. When she put her foot to the ground, she winced with the sharpness of the pain that ran like a sword through her ankle.

"I was seeking shelter," she said, and he had to bend his head to catch the words. "I fell, as I ran to the gate. I did not see the ditch."

He looked at her muddied skirt, and nodded. The trickle of blood came from a small cut on her forehead where she had struck a sharp stone in falling, and her ankle was swollen.

It was no easy matter to lift her on to Dandy's back, and he thanked God for his physical strength; but he was panting when at last it was accomplished, and she was in front of him in the saddle, almost a dead weight as she leant against him. There was no lessening of the rain, as he began the short journey that now seemed incredibly long; when they turned in at the gates of Russington, he was as wet as she was, and he felt exhausted.

One of the servants came running out, openmouthed with astonishment, as he reached the house; carefully he slid his burden down into the waiting arms.

"Send Nanny Gaunt to me," he ordered. "And get a groom for my horse. See that one of the rooms upstairs is made ready, with a bed and linen, and towels and hot water."

He strode into the house, flinging down his wet cloak; Nanny Gaunt hurried to him, wearing a ludicrous look of amazement that would have amused him at any other time. He repeated his instructions to her, seeing the curiosity in her face, as she turned and hurried up the wide, shallow curve of stairs.

Taroola by this time lay like a rag doll on the settle where she had been placed, eyes closed, her face the colour of the parchment on which his maps were printed. Gently, he eased away the cloak; the thin, clinging muslin dress outlined every curve of her lissom figure. She was, he thought, with complete detachment, beautifully made. He scooped her up in his arms, and her eyes flickered open again, vaguely, as he carried her up the stairs and laid her down on the bed, for the ministrations of Nanny and the wide-eyed servant girls. Then he went to his own room and changed into dry clothing; overhead, the thunder boomed like cannon. It sounded like Waterloo, he thought, remembering the horror and carnage of the bitterly-fought battle. Lightning blinked in the wake of the thunder, and, from the window of his room, he saw branches torn from the trees and whipped along savagely by the wind. It was a bad storm, a high fee for the long, hot days they had enjoyed.

In the big, high-ceilinged room above him, Nanny and the maids stripped off the wet clothing and dried Taroola with rough, warm towels, before they put on an old flannel nightgown that belonged to Nanny. Nanny dressed the cut on her forehead, and put a cold compress on the swelling ankle; Taroola scarcely stirred, only moaned and shivered, and looked at them occasionally, as though they had come from another world. When the coverlets were finally pulled over her, she slept as though she had not closed her eyes for weeks.

Nanny stood looking down at her, hands on her hips, lips pursed. A lady, she thought; no doubt as to that. Gently born, and with breeding in her face. It was a good face, to which Nanny had taken an instant liking. *That* was what was lacking in the face of that green-eyed little Madam at Roxton Hall, Nanny decided; breeding. Fine clothes would never make a fine lady of *her*.

She went downstairs to where he waited impatiently.

"Well?" he said.

"She is asleep, Master Philip. I have dressed her

head and there is a great swelling on her foot; she seems like to sleep for hours. Exhausted, poor creature. Shame on you, sir, for allowing her to leave, *on foot,* with such a storm brewing!"

"I did no such thing, Nanny!" he replied tartly. "It was at her own wish. A wilful young woman, I assure you, who insisted that she preferred to return to the Inn alone rather than accept the offer of my carriage or my company."

Nanny folded her hands over her apron, waiting; he told her briefly of his first meeting with Taroola at the sheep station beyond the Blue Mountains. Nanny said calmly:

"I recognize the ring she wears on her finger. 'Tes Master Richard's, the one he has had since he was a young man. Ah well, that is no mystery. No doubt he gave it to her, with promises that he never meant to keep."

Philip's silence was confirmation; he stared out of the window at the rain-sodden landscape, frowning. He had never looked so aloof and arrogant, so much master of Russington, she thought. Not a man with whom to cross swords, if he believed he had right on his side. But a just man, honest, proud, she admitted. A pity the young lady who slept under his roof had eyes only for a pretty charmer like Richard.

The thunder was edging away, the rain thinning to a fine, peevish drizzle.

"Miss Brandon will be staying here," he told Nanny. "In the state she is in, she cannot be moved for some days. Send one of the servants to the Inn to collect her belongings and bring them here. Do you think it necessary for the physician to be called?"

"No, sir!" Nanny protested, indignant and affronted. "I have dealt with her injuries and she will suffer no more than a chill. What use have we for physicians with their fa-las and new-fangled ideas?"

But the next two days proved that Taroola had suffered more than a chill taken from the storm. That night when Nanny Gaunt carried a bowl of broth to her, she scarcely sipped it, and lay back against the pillows, her flesh dry and burning, her eyes over-bright, and asked vaguely why Richard did not come. Nanny took the news to Philip, next morning, that she was no better; there was high fever and she breathed with difficulty; so a servant was despatched to Quinton St. John with instructions to bring back a physician with all speed. The man he brought was a good one.

In his opinion, he said, the young lady was suffering from a fever, as a result of the exposure, and she should be nursed night and day; he did not know what Philip, who had some medical knowledge, strongly suspected: that the shock of discovering Richard was married had been too much for Taroola, aggravating the fever that shook her like a storm.

Nanny sat with her night and day, nursing her devotedly; Taroola opened her eyes occasionally, looking around the room as though trying to locate where she was; she asked repeatedly for Richard, and her talk showed clearly that her affections were still centred in him, in spite of the broken promise he had given her. Sometimes she cried piteously for him; at others she talked of strange places and things to which Nanny listened in wonderment: of the sheep station, the wild and beautiful mountains, her father, the strange black people she saw; she spoke of the times she had talked to Richard, her anger that he had been falsely accused, the brief, sweet, secret meetings. Nanny shook her head, sorrowfully, piecing the picture together, and thinking that Miss Brandon had not had an easy time of it, by all accounts, coming all this way, after her father's death, to find her love married to someone else. Young women these days had no sense, Nanny thought, exasperated; what she could see in such a weakling, Heaven alone knew.

On the third day after Taroola had been brought to Russington, Esther Roxton drove over in her carriage;

strange rumours had filtered through to her, relayed by Hawkins, her maid, who found it rewarding to bring every bit of gossip to her mistress, for she was handsomely repaid by gifts; thus did Esther ensure that she was kept informed of all happenings both at Roxton and at Russington.

She was perturbed; not because it was said that the woman in Philip's house had come in search of Richard, but that she should be there at all. Things had not gone entirely as she had foreseen during the six months of her marriage. It had been more difficult than she imagined to bend Richard to her will, in spite of her threats; well, the time was coming when she would implement those threats with action. How easy it would be to put him out of the way forever! She closed her eyes and leant back against the carriage seat, happily contemplating her status as the widowed Lady Roxton; but she was not entirely at ease. There were snags she had not foreseen. Her passion for Philip that grew each time she saw him, and was the more intense because it must remain temporarily unsatisfied, had changed certain aspects of the situation for her.

She saw herself denouncing Richard; in her mind she had already set the scene. Herself, proud, sorrowful, but determined that justice should be done, handing over the damning documents to the authorities, knowing that retribution would be swift and absolute. But how would Philip react, she had begun to wonder uneasily? He had never figured in her original calculations, because he had not existed before the time Richard had presented her to him. Would Philip feel she should have shielded his kinsman, not denounced him, would he see her as a vengeful, vindictive woman, making away with a husband who had made a mockery of marriage?

Be that as it may, she thought determinedly, it had to be done. She would send for the documents, tell Mr. Peach to bring them himself from the dusty, sleazy lawyer's office in London where he held them in safe cus-

tody for her; the sooner the better. She had stayed her
hand this length of time because it seemed more
decorous. Her story that she had found the documents
amongst papers belonging to Sir Thomas would be
good enough. She had never cared what the world
might think of her action in betraying Richard, but she
did care very much what Philip might think. She
frowned, pondering upon the news that had filtered
through from Russington; so it was in a thoughtful
frame of mind that she arrived, to be greeted by Philip.

She knew she looked her best, in a dress of stiff, rich
material, that matched her eyes, her hair coiled and
brushed vigorously by Hawkins until it shone like silk.
There was colour in her cheeks and a sparkle in her
eyes, as always when she was near Philip; she sat, a
small, upright figure, on the brocaded couch in the
drawing-room and said gaily:

"Well, Philip? Strange rumours have reached me! It
seems that you have abducted a young woman!"

His eyebrows lifted and he smiled.

"Scarcely that! The young woman in question is ill
and alone in this country; and I had given her father
my word that I would offer her whatever help and protection she might need."

"Oh?" Her voice was pert. "Then you were expect-
ing her to come to you?"

"No." He hesitated, unwilling to discuss Taroola, but
knowing full well to what extent servants gossiped; he
did not doubt that Esther already knew most of the
story. He told her what had happened on the station,
leaving out the fact that Taroola wore Richard's ring;
but at the conclusion of his brief, guarded tale, Esther
said calmly:

"You have no idea what sharp eyes servants possess,
Philip; I am told she wears a ring with the Roxton coat
of arms upon it."

"Yes," he admitted briefly.

"By whom was it given?"

He frowned, seeing no way out; and when he was silent, she said gently:

"Come, Philip, I can guess. Richard gave it to her, no doubt with a promise to wed her. How loyal you are to your Cousin!" Her eyes filled with the tears that came so easily. "How ill he deserves it, I fear. He has placed you in a most unfortunate position."

"Why?" Philip demanded.

She looked down at the hands folded in her lap, and said delicately:

"You are a bachelor, Philip; she is young, and, by all accounts, a most attractive woman. There is bound to be gossip."

"She has no liking for me," he retorted, "and, for my part, I have no designs upon her. People will say what they will; I care only that I have kept my word to her father."

His voice was forbidding, but Esther breathed a sigh of relief; she had the information she wanted. Philip was apparently not enamoured of the woman who lay upstairs; nevertheless, proximity was often a dangerous thing.

"What are you going to do?" she asked. "Nanny will nurse her back to health; but you say she does not intend to seek out relatives living in this country. Very well, then—what is to happen? Will she throw herself upon your mercy, for you to provide a home her here, rather than return alone to Australia?"

She realized she had gone too far; Philip's forbidding frown stated clearly that he was capable of managing his own affairs without help from anyone. His very look—dark, aloof—made small threads of fire run through her veins. When he said nothing, she added placatingly:

"I have trespassed, Philip; I beg you to believe that such trespass comes only from concern for your welfare, as you have shown concern for mine."

It was prettily put and earned her his forgiveness; his

face relaxed a little, and he said pleasantly:

"Time enough to decide such issues when she is stronger. She has fever and delirium, as a result of the soaking she endured, and she has but recently lost her father."

"Also," said Esther shrewdly, "it undoubtedly shocked her greatly to discover that Richard had been false to her. Poor child! Forgive me, Philip! You have been a great comfort to me, and if I am over-zealous for you, it, is perhaps understandable. I find the situation at Roxton both unhappy and difficult. I am alarmed at the way in which Richard squanders money that should be turned to better account."

"You are a sensible woman, Esther; but even you cannot saddle a mule, I fear!" Philip said drily.

Sensible! She fidgeted beneath the word; it was, suddenly, not the way she wanted Philip to see her at all. She thought of the girl named Anne Brandon; Philip York was the kind of man who would provide for her, keep her permanently at Russington if she had nowhere else to go, Esther thought, in sudden panic. It was high time something was resolved; the sooner she sent for Augustus Peach, the better.

Richard was astounded to hear that Taroola was at Russington; he rode over to his cousin's at once. Philip greeted him coldly, and he was perturbed. God knows, he thought furiously, I have enough trouble without *this!* Esther had confronted him with the story, and taunted him with the fact that Taroola was wearing his ring. A pretty tale it would make, as she had pointed out. Already, he was known to be a profligate, a man of debauched tastes who satisfied them with what dubious company he could find in London! Now, one of his abandoned mistresses was almost on his doorstep!

He had let the tirade flow over him, indifferent to her sneers; she watched him with her cold green eyes and contemplated the coming of Augustus Peach with a great deal of satisfaction. She did not want Richard to know how soon she planned to denounce him, for then he might go to ground, even flee the country, if he had enough warning of her intentions; she wanted him safely in the net, brought to Tyburn. Nothing else would do. So she waited with what patience she could muster, despatched her instructions to London, and amused herself by driving round the estate, Sebastian at her side, a delightful picture of maternal solicitude. And all the while she promised herself that soon these lands would be hers, in trust for her son.

"I bear no responsibility for James Brandon's daughter!" Richard told his cousin.

"No!" Philip said coldly. "I view the matter differently; she has the protection of my roof and my help for so long as she requires it!"

"That is a matter for your conscience!" Richard smiled sourly at him, a knowing look on his face. "No doubt you will find her rewarding company! If you have never taken a woman to bed, Philip, you do not know what pleasures you have foregone!"

Philip's look of distaste and anger amused him; it was a joy to see his cousin so put out, he thought! And then he fell to reflecting, moodily, that his life might have been a great deal more bearable had he stayed in Australia and wed this woman who was probably wealthy. He thought yearningly of the freedom that would have been his; how ironic life was! Esther's threats had become more violent of late and he knew that he could not bear the uncertainty of his position much longer. He had supposed that once they were married she would docilely yield up the document and he would then be able to free himself of her forever; since that assumption had been proved wrong, he had formulated and discarded a dozen grandiose schemes for killing her. It would not be easy; she was shrewd and watchful of him, and he knew it must look like an accident. Better, first, to find out where she had hidden the documents; but he had searched every nook and cranny of the house, every personal item of hers, and had not found them. His one thought was to find them soon, before it was too late. He distrusted Esther, uneasily aware that she could make the shadow of Tyburn become a substantial reality, any time she chose.

Several days later, Taroola lay against the pillows in her room, weak but quite lucid in her mind, remembering all that had happened since the ship that had brought her to England had docked. She wore her own nightclothes; her hair had been brushed by Nanny and tied back from a face grown thinner and pale, but still very lovely, the eyes the colour of the sea on a summer day. Nanny's kindly ministrations had earned a gratitude that Taroola had expressed freely, to the old servant's immense delight; but she felt weariness, lassitude, and a sense of desolation. She was alone; she knew no one here, save Richard, who had rejected her. Carefully, she took his ring from her finger and placed it on the table beside her bed; she was dependent upon the hospitality of a man she disliked, Philip York, the arrogant, overbearing master of Russington, now on his way upstairs to see her.

He came to the foot of the bed and looked down at her gravely; he seemed to fill the room, he was so tall, so full of a strength and vitality that was more than physical. His dark eyes beneath their thick brows gave away none of his secrets, the full mouth was as firmly disciplined as it had always been, his dark hair grew thick and curling, and, she admitted freely, he was immensely attractive; but not to her.

"I am glad that you are recovering," he said formally.

"Thank you." Her voice was distant. "I have encroached too long upon your hospitality, I fear."

"I have neither said nor thought so," he pointed out curtly.

"Nevertheless, it *is* so," she insisted; she yielded nothing to him except an unwilling acceptance of favours received, he thought angrily. He saw the misery in her eyes and knew that she still grieved for Richard.

"I cannot stay here," she pointed out. "I have no wish to be an embarrassment to Richard."

"So you are still sick with love for him!" he said contemptuously.

It was an unkind remark, he knew; but he would not withdraw it, though he saw her flinch from its truth.

She replied coldly: "I am well able to recompense you for whatever debts I have incurred and I thank you for what you have done for me; but my feelings for Richard are my concern."

She knew it was unforgivable. Hurt for hurt, that was what it was. But—*sick with love,* he had said. She was still weak and the tears glittered in her eyes; she saw the colour burn in his cheeks, and knew how deeply she had insulted him. She did not care; he had rescued her, brought her here, had her looked after and she had struck, deliberately, at his pride. She, who had never been afraid of any man, was ashamed and half-afraid of what she had done, seeing him there, tall, cold-eyed, contemptuous.

"I gave your father a promise to help you," he retorted. "I have fulfilled it to the best of my ability. Should you need my help again, you will ask for it, madam! You have a viper's tongue!"

He went angrily from the room; she lay back against the pillows and wept, knowing it would be some time yet before she would be strong enough to leave. Well, at least she would not have to see much of Mr. Philip York; and if she might see Richard just once, then she would ask no more.

Downstairs in his study, Philip picked up his quill to compose a letter to his lawyers. He had little enough to go on: James and Mary Brandon. James had mentioned relations in Kent. That was all he knew, and if he DID succeed in tracing her relatives, Taroola would not thank him; but he could not turn her adrift without anyone to care for her, he reflected.

Nanny, who had heard Taroola repeatedly call Richard's name through her delirium, reminded herself repeatedly that it was no business of hers if Miss Brandon was foolish enough not to see how poorly Richard compared with his cousin; but she put her point across subtly, praising Philip and all he did for the people in his care. Taroola remained politely indifferent, but she liked Nanny, so she said nothing. On the day that she came downstairs for the first time, Nanny surprised her by asking her if she felt well enough to entertain a visitor.

"Who is it?" Taroola asked.

"Old Lady Roxton, miss. Sir Richard's mother. She has heard that Mr. York has a visitor who is sick," she added, with rare tact, "and has been most concerned. Pour soul, she has little enough to occupy her time. She has not been herself since Master Richard was sent to Australia, and then when old Sir Thomas died, so sudden, why it was no wonder the poor woman became a little strange. She is simple and quite harmless, and most interesting to talk to, for she knows all the local history; but her mind goes back, you see. She thinks that Mr. Philip and Sir Richard are boys again, at school and that her husband is away; it is better so, perhaps. She does not see things as we do, but who is to say she is not happier in her own world?"

Taroola took an instant liking to the tall woman with the untidy grey hair and vague eyes, who greeted her so kindly. She found a certain sad pleasure in talking with Richard's mother, hearing tales of when the two cousins were boys. Eleanor Roxton spoke quite lucidly of the accident that had robbed Philip of his family.

"He was eighteen at the time, a fine lad, like his mother in looks. His mother and his father and his little sister Katherine had gone to visit friends. Katherine was twelve years old, such a pretty little creature, and Philip doted on her. Philip stayed at home because he had been ill; but he was much better, he insisted, well enough to walk down to the bridge and meet them on their way home. It was spring, there had been heavy rains, and the river was in full flood; the bridge was an old wooden one, near the point where two rivers join; but it was sound enough, everyone said." Lady Roxton nodded sadly. "He was waiting there, and no one knows what happened. It may have been a rabbit or some small creature who ran under the horses' hooves frightening them, so that they reared up in terror, and the coach crashed through the side of the bridge into the river. They were swept away and drowned. Poor Philip was nearly demented; he dived in after them and all but lost his own life. He was half-dead when they pulled him out, wedged between two rocks." She nodded again, her mind slipping its leash, as she added sadly:

"Poor Richard will be so upset to hear of the death of his Aunt and Uncle and his little cousin. He will be home for the holidays soon now. . . ."

Taroola felt a stab of pity for Philip; it was a terrible thing to have happened to a boy of eighteen, she thought.

Eleanor's talk of Richard's wife surprised and disconcerted Taroola.

"Richard says she has come to stay with us, and we must make ourselves agreeable to her," Lady Eleanor confided, almost in a whisper, nervously tucking back straying strands of hair, her eyes moving restlessly about the room. "I have heard her speak most sharply and unkindly to Richard, when the servants are not about; and she speaks to me as though I were a child who should be slapped. Indeed, she once slapped me! It was most *disgraceful!* I wish that my husband was at home, for he would know how to deal with her. I am sure he would not allow her to stay, Miss Brandon. She

is most secretive and strange; she will not let me into
the nursery to play with her son. And I do so enjoy the
ways of little children. Not that he is an amiable child,
for he has a strong will of his own and when he is
thwarted he shrieks with temper fit to split one's head
with the noise!"

Eleanor put her hands to her head, as though to
stress the point; Taroola was troubled, and felt relieved
when the old lady began to talk of the elm that had
fallen in the churchyard on the day of the storm.

There had been trouble in the village; Richard, for
once, was compelled to put in an appearance, to face a
group of angry tenants demanding that something
should be done to make their cottages habitable. A
baby had died from the damp that seeped in through
walls and roofs, when the small, dark rooms had been
awash during the recent storm. Since then, the anger
and resentment had grown to formidable proportions.
The Home Farm Piggeries were better places to live in
than their hovels, they declared, and even Sir Richard's
prize herd of cattle had dry barns and good fodder. He
had made promises to them that he had not kept. What
was he going to do about it?

Richard had looked at them, standing surly and unsmiling, with their staves and their pitchforks, and
known the queasiness of panic in his stomach. He
made the promises over again, with charm, with vehe-
mence, with an assurance that left them unconvinced;
he rode home with frantic haste, anxious to be free of
them and their demands, wondering where in God's
name he would find the money for all he had promised.
Esther did not believe him when he told her there was
little enough left, and the rents his tenants paid were
barely sufficient to support her extravagant housekeep-
ing. Well, she would soon find out for herself; as for
him, he thought wildly, there might be, after all, a way
of escape. Taroola. He could persuade her to help him
leave the country, with her. He would be free for ever

of Esther, in spite of her boasts of being able to find him, no matter where he went; free of the house and lands that hung a millstone around his neck, of the child over whom Esther fussed so nauseatingly, free of everything that hampered and hindered his enjoyment of life. Taroola would be pleasant company after Esther, he thought sourly.

He was in a black mood when Esther came to the library to him, before dinner. She looked down at him with a hatred tempered by the fact that the long waiting was almost over. She knew very well where he would go, after dinner, and whom he would be with; she made it her business to find out all these things. Let him go, she thought contemptuously! Everyone knew what he was; by his actions he put a noose around his neck, a more intangible one, true, than the thick rope at Tyburn, but nonetheless as useful.

"Tomorrow evening," she said coldly, "we shall have guests; including a friend of mine from London: Mr. Peach. And also your cousin Philip and Miss Brandon. Ah! That surprises you!" She smiled at his startled look. "I confess I had difficulty in persuading Philip to accept the invitation, and he was most dubious on behalf of Miss Brandon, but I have had word that she will accompany him. No doubt she is as curious to see me as I am to see her. I persuaded him that to invite her was a gesture of friendliness on my part that would silence any gossiping tongues; he thinks most highly of my kindness!" She began to laugh, triumphantly.

"Would that I had stayed in Australia with her!" he said morosely.

"I do not think Miss Brandon's father would have accepted a convict son-in-law. Well, Richard? You are prepared to make yourself agreeable tomorrow evening, I have no doubt?" she said gaily.

"For Miss Brandon—yes!" he said softly, enjoying the way her eyes narrowed at his taunt. "You have your own diversions, it seems. This Mr. Peach. I have never heard of him."

"He is a friend of the late Mr. Caldecott," she said smoothly. "He looks after Sebastian's interests."

"Caldecott!" He spat the name, with a scornful laughter, at her. "On your own admission, he never existed."

"I also said that I found his name useful. His presence need not concern you."

Richard was thinking too much of his coming encounter with Taroola to pay much heed to Mr. Augustus Peach. Time, as well as distance, had lent enchantment to his view of her. He would tell her his father had forced him into marriage with Esther. Sudden desire rose in him; when dinner was over, he ordered the carriage and drove into Quinton St. John; in a good mood, he tossed the coachman some money and told him to come back in a couple of hours, then he made his way to the dark back streets where Bessie Lowndes lived in a narrow, untidy little house; she was a farm labourer's daughter, who had found there were better ways of getting a living than making lace or scrubbing floors. She was a big woman, comely, soft as a feather pillow, quick to sense a mood, and full of humour. She never asked questions, nor pretended not to know what her customers came seeking.

She took him to her bed, and when their love-making was over, she lit the candle and watched him lying beside her, relaxed. Richard looked at the heavy body, soft, smooth, white; and let out a long sigh.

"Let's have some food, and something to drink, Bessie," he coaxed.

"Hungry, are you?" She smiled knowingly and got up from the tumbled bed, groping for a wrapper; he watched, with sly amusement, her efforts to confine her enormous bosoms inside the thin material. She had beautiful hands, he thought absently.

"Yours are a lady's hands, Bessie!" he teased. "White as snow!"

The compliment pleased her; but she protested, good-humouredly, that her hands worked hard enough.

"It's arsenic keeps them white," she told him knowingly. "Good for the skin. That's a woman's trick, not one you'd know. Like the herbs for the hair."

She went heavily from the room; Richard lay watching the long shadows from the guttering candle, climb and dance on the walls; and he thought of tomorrow, clutching, as he always did, at anything that offered him a way of escape from harsh reality.

CHAPTER FIVE

Augustus Peach arrived late the following afternoon; Lady Eleanor saw his arrival, and wondered who he was; she did not like the look of him at all. She was feeling very put out because her daughter-in-law had made it clear that she did not wish Eleanor to be present at this evening's dinner. She must take her meal in her room, Esther insisted; she embarrassed guests by her insistence on living twenty years in the past.

Eleanor was resentful; when she had complained to Richard, he had merely shrugged indifferently, and said she would probably be a deal more comfortable on her own, anyway. She was querulous, angry, feeling vaguely slighted in some way, and her resentment centred on Esther, like a swarm of bees, because nothing had been the same since she had come to Roxton.

And this Mr. Peach. She wondered about him; something was afoot. She was going to keep an eye on him, and on Esther. Eleanor nodded determinedly to herself; she had a vague premonition, a sharpening of her senses where Richard was concerned; this man meant some ill. She was sure of it. She must be careful, she told herself solemnly; not let them guess. It was her duty to protect her son and her husband from any possible harm.

Mr. Peach looked as though he might crumble into

dust at a touch; a small, wizened man in his fifties, with a creased, papery face, shiny black hair brushed close to his bony head, and small, hard black eyes, very alert. When Richard saw him, he wondered, scornfully, if this was some cast-off lover of Esther's.

Esther poured tea for Augustus in the long drawing-room.

"You have brought what I requested?" she asked softly.

"Of course," he replied reproachfully. "Your instructions were most precise, madam."

She nodded, satisfied.

"Very well. We shall not discuss it nor conduct our business here. After tea, I shall show you the Roxton portraits in the Gallery, and then we will go to a place in this house where we can be sure of not having eaves-droppers or other disturbances; you will then give me the package."

He looked at her covertly. A strange secretive woman; he remembered when she had first come to him; she looked a good deal more prosperous, these days. Done nicely for herself, he thought, and he would have given a lot to know the contents of the package she had deposited with his firm for safe keeping; they must be important to justify her paying his expenses for this overnight visit. He had not dared to open it—it was very carefully wrapped and heavily sealed with a small crest on every circle of wax. He knew quite well that she would examine each seal when he handed her the small packet that felt like papers. Letters of some kind; blackmail, no doubt. Well, it was her affair, and he had been handsomely paid for keeping the packet in his safe all this time, he reflected.

"I should be delighted to see the Picture Gallery, Lady Roxton," he said smoothly.

Lady Eleanor watched them from the far end of the gallery, half-hidden by thick velvet drapes at the window; she was excited, cheeks flushed, eyes bright. The part she was acting gave her a feeling of importance. It was just like playing hide-and-seek with Richard. How he loved that game! They would play it tomorrow, perhaps when he was not busy.

Esther and Mr. Peach almost brushed against her, as they passed close by, and excitement quivered within her; her heart beat fast, she was quite breathless with the strain of it all, but she must *watch*. . . .

She moved with cunning and stealth, her soft kid slippers making no sound on the thick carpets. Nearly all the servants were downstairs, preparing for the elaborate dinner Lady Roxton was giving; so she hid and followed, and was astonished to see that Esther finally led her guest up a very short flight of steps.

The steps led to what was a small cul-de-sac containing only two rooms. The larger one was Richard's old nursery and no one *ever* went there now except herself, Eleanor thought indignantly. Certainly not Esther, who had inspected it briefly when she first came to Roxton; she had a large room near her own suite made into a nursery for Sebastian; it had been elaborately furnished and a new nursemaid installed.

Sudden triumph glimmered in Eleanor's vague blue eyes; she knew all about *this* room—and the adjoining one, which contained a great many things that were not used any more; she knew the secrets of the old Nursery, for had not Richard once played a joke on her, frightening her half to death, by climbing into the cupboard that backed on to the wall of the Nursery, hiding there whilst they searched the house for him—and then showing her, triumphantly, the small knot hole in the panelling to which an eye could be applied, giving a good view of all that was happening in the room beyond?

She watched the Nursery door close behind Mr. Peach and Esther; like a small shadow she tiptoed past the old Nursery door, opened the door of the adjoining room, and closed it soundlessly behind her. Through the years, the unwanted objects had accumulated here, and she had to pick her way carefully over them to reach the cupboard. She was afraid the door would creak; she must not be caught, for that would spoil the game. . . .

The door of the big cupboard gave easily; she stepped cautiously inside, and found the knot hole without much difficulty. . . .

They were talking very quietly; she could scarcely hear a word. Mr. Peach was handing a small packet to Esther; she was examining it very carefully, then she lifted her head, and nodded, telling him that his fee would be paid him before he left. Her nod was a gesture of dismissal, and she sent Mr. Peach on his way. Evidently, she was giving him instructions as to how to reach his own room again.

"There is no need," Esther said coolly, "for anyone present this evening to be aware that yours is other than a friendly visit to give me certain advice. I do not wish the package mentioned, you understand?"

"Naturally," he replied, ruffled, because she seemed quite unaware of his long experience of being discreet and keeping secrets.

When he had gone, she turned the packet over and over in her hands, as though she yearned to open it; she smiled triumphantly, a smile that Eleanor did not like at all. Then she looked thoughtfully at the room. It contained a beautifully carved desk that, like the abandoned Noah's Ark and painted hobby horse, had been made by the local carpenter; an old toy fort, a set of red-coated soldiers, a splendid sailing ship with torn sails, books, a dozen reminders of Richard's childhood. Her glance rested finally on the life-size rocking-horse with his flaring nostrils and horsehair tail, his bright wooden body, and leather reins; this, too, was the work of the local carpenter, and had a beautiful leather saddle upon its back, an exact replica of a life-sized one.

Esther pondered a moment; then she loosened the girth, lifted the saddle and slid the packet beneath it between the painted wooden body and the leather, carefully readjusting straps and saddle. She was laughing softly to herself as she left the room, she locked the door behind her.

Eleanor was in the throes of an almost unbearable excitement. Did she think to keep *me* out of *Richard's* nursery, she wondered angrily? She does not know how often *I* come here to touch his toys and remind myself that he will soon be back to play with them again! Eleanor's laughter was as soft and triumphant as Esther's had been as her fingers searched along the cupboard wall and found the spare key that had been hidden there since the day Richard had locked himself inside his Nursery in a fit of temper. . . .

Whatever was in the packet, Esther seemed to set great store by it. The heightened perception that she always felt where her son was concerned, prodded Eleanor into activity. Esther must not be allowed to keep the strange package which seemed to please her so much. It is not safe for her to have it, thought Eleanor.

Philip had been surprised that Taroola had agreed to attend the dinner at Roxton Hall; but he thought she had accepted only because she longed to see Richard again. Richard had not called to see her, neither had she left Russington since the day Philip had brought her there.

She and Philip usually avoided one another; it was not difficult. Occasionally they dined together but conversation between them was stilted and Taroola and he were not at ease with one another. Usually, she took a tray, alone in her room. By day she walked in the gardens, unaware how often Philip watched her from his study window. He was extremely busy; Taroola endured Nanny Gaunt's continual praise-singing of Philip's goodness to his tenants, with as much patience as she could muster, and largely because Nanny had been kind to her. She disliked the master of Russington intensely, but her heartbeats quickened excitedly at the thought of the invitation to Roxton; nothing would have kept her away.

On the evening of the dinner, she came down to the drawing-room at the precise hour Philip had named; he was waiting for her, staring down into the heat of the flames, for a log fire had been lighted against the unexpected chill of an evening that warned of summer's coming departure.

He turned slowly, and caught his breath when he saw her. She looked very beautiful, her hair dressed simply but exquisitely by Nanny; she wore a dress of some yellow material, neither fashionable nor elaborate, but it reminded him of sunshine and buttercups in a meadow. With her creamy skin and dark red hair, the effect was superb. She wore little jewellery, but he recognized its value: an old Spanish brooch of gold set with diamonds and topaz, matching earrings, a ring with a stone that flashed yellow fire, on her right hand.

Seen against the background of the drawing-room, she made the kind of picture he would gladly have commissioned an artist to transmit to canvas. He thought, for the first time, how it would be to have a woman like that in his house, always. A young woman; love, warmth, laughter, children. Deliberately he closed his mind to the thought; he had never loved a woman. All his energies had been put to work amongst the people his father had cared so much about, and he had no taste for light-hearted affairs with willing young women.

He merely said:

"Were you carrying those jewels amongst your luggage that was brought here from the Inn?"

"Yes," she said, with cool surprise. "Why do you ask?"

"It was a risky business to carry such valuables with

you. Did it not occur to you that you might be robbed?"

"No," she said, with perfect truth. "These were my mother's. Her other jewellery I have deposited for safe keeping with my father's lawyers in Sydney. Like these, they are of value to me only because they belonged to her."

She sat stiffly beside Philip during the short journey to Roxton; he was aware of her nearness in a way that made him uneasy. The moon was up, round and full and the countryside flowed with liquid silver. Somewhere, an owl hooted with a sad sound; the faint creaking of the coach, and the rhythm of the horses' hooves were the only other sounds in the late summer night.

"A night for highwaymen," he said.

"Highwaymen?" she sounded surprised. "What are they?"

He remembered that she had grown up in Australia where the business of robbing travellers was less romantically conducted; he told her, and for good measure added tales of smuggling, of the brandy and lace and tobacco that were brought in by boats sliding smoothly into quiet coves, when the weather was right and the moon did not betray the crews. She listened interestedly, thinking that he had quite a gift for words; but by this time, they were turning into the gates of Roxton Park, and she leaned forward eagerly to get a better view of the vast bulk of the lighted house, clearly visible in the moonlight, the parkland around it imprinted with sharp black shadows. Philip heard her quick, indrawn breath; so she was impressed, he thought scornfully. Or was it excitement at the thought of seeing Richard again?

Taroola had fiercely commanded herself to remain mistress of the situation, but she knew all her defences would crumble when she saw Richard; when the man-servant held open the great doors and she walked proudly into Roxton Hall, though her hands trembled.

For Esther Roxton, it was to be a glittering occasion; she had invited a score of people from the county, and although she knew full well that most of them would come out of sheer curiosity, nevertheless, the idea of herself as hostess at Roxton always gave her a tremendous sense of power. They did not entertain half often enough or on a lavish enough scale, she reflected; well, it would be different when Richard was no longer master there. Let them come to look at the widow with the young son who had lived quietly in Quinton St. John before her marriage; let them stare and wonder and speculate! She would enjoy it! And tonight, Philip was coming; the blood quickened in her veins, her pulses raced. As for the girl who was coming with him, she was probably a plain little creature, as interesting as a cup of gruel; she had no fears on *her* account!

The manservant announced them, and Esther moved forward, in her stiff, expensive dress with its elaborate trimming and the jewels she had purloined for herself from Eleanor's casket. She looked, beside Taroola, like a small, green parakeet; fussy, over-dressed. She was shrewd enough to recognize that fact, as soon as she saw the girl with Philip; fury rose like a black tide within her. This *chit,* she thought bitterly, made every woman in the room look old or too elaborate! Standing there, smiling, beside Philip, further inflaming Esther, so that her hands shook and she could scarcely compose herself. Had Philip found her irresistible, she wondered? The picture of him acting as protector to a penniless little waif from the other side of the world was gone forever; she would see to it that Russington was rid of this witch as soon as possible, for if the girl was not already Philip's mistress, then she soon would be.

"My dear Miss Brandon!" she said charmingly. "I am so delighted that you are with us, this evening. I know that Mr. York has been taking good care of you." She turned to Richard.

"Richard, you know Miss Brandon already," she said softly.

Taroola looked at Esther; at the emerald green eyes with their strange glitter, the white skin, the rouged cheeks, the hard mouth. She shivered, as though ice, not blood, ran in her veins; then she looked at Richard, and thought she would faint. He looked as blond, as handsome as ever, with that faintly petulant look more marked. In the long hours when she had been alone at Russington she had told herself over and over again that her love for him was dead. Now she knew that it was not so; seeing him, standing beside his wife, great bitterness and pain welled up within her.

Esther drew Philip aside.

"How long will Miss Brandon be with you, Philip?" she asked softly.

He shrugged. "I believe she is as anxious to be rid of me as I am to see her gone."

"Oh, Philip, that is ungallant of you!" she chided playfully.

All through the long, elaborate dinner, Philip watched them; they were not seated close enough to one another to make intimate conversation; but each look spoke for them. Reproach, longing, love, on Taroola's part; a slow rousing of passion on Richard's.

After dinner there was dancing and card-games for those who were too infirm or who did not wish to dance. The ballroom had been decorated with flowers and greenery; when Philip would have led Taroola on to the floor, she said quietly:

"I regret that my education in Australia has not prepared me for an English ballroom, Mr. York. I am unable to dance."

"The steps are not difficult," he said shortly. "I will teach you."

She shook her head; Philip shrugged; so she did not want him to partner her, he thought? Very well! From the corner of his eye, he saw Richard come across; he moved sharply away, knowing Richard would claim Taroola; later they left the ballroom. Esther looked at them with amused eyes; well, let him have his pleasure of her, she thought scornfully! Let them all see how I am slighted by my husband.

Philip watched them leave the ballroom, with a feeling of deep disgust. He knew that Taroola was his cousin's mistress, but did they both have to advertise the fact so blatantly?

"I must speak alone with you!" Richard whispered urgently to Taroola, in the ballroom.

"Richard, we *cannot!* To be seen leaving with you would invite comment!" she replied unhappily. "And we have no reason, now, to speak alone! It has all been said, long since!"

"But you are wrong!" His voice was compelling. *"Please!* I beg you! There is much I must say to you. I would have come to Russington, long since, but for that watchdog of a cousin of mine, who hinted most plainly that I would be unwelcome at his house so long as you remained there!"

Against her will, Taroola allowed herself to be persuaded to leave the ballroom with Richard; they stepped out on to the terrace, and he led her down a flight of steps, through the moon-silvered garden, to a small marble temple that gleamed behind a screen of dark yew and clipped cypress. Inside the temple he caught her to him with a suddenness that took her breath away; she shook her head vehemently.

"No, Richard, *no!*" she whispered. "Do you forget that your wife is in *there,* in that house you share together? The house of which you often spoke to me? Or have you forgotten, even as you forgot the promises you made before you left my father's house in Australia?" She pulled an arm free and opened the reticule she carried; from it, she took a small gold ring which she held out to him.

"This is yours, Richard! All our talking is done for-ever! Let us go back to the house!" she cried.

"Why did you come to England?" he demanded.

"Because I had heard nothing from you. No word;

and you did not return. I feared some harm had come to you; when I learnt of your marriage, I believed that my ears played tricks. Your cousin confirmed the truth. We have nothing to speak about!"

She turned away, her eyes full of tears, but he caught hold of her, making her look at him.

"You are wrong!" he told her. "My marriage is nothing but a millstone around my neck, a mistake, bondage to a woman who is cold and greedy and cruel."

"Then why did you marry her?" she demanded impatiently.

"It was my father's wish!" he lied. "Before he died, he made it clear to me that he thought Esther would make me an excellent and sensible wife!"

"Nonsense, Richard! Are you a child without will of your own!" she retorted incredulously.

She looked bewildered and disbelieving, confronting him in the moonlight that lay in silver stripes across the floor; her anger, her proximity, the reappraisal of the beauty that had faded in his mind, during the past year, made him desire her with a frenzy that he found hard to control; but he was cautious only because he remembered the night at the sheep station when she had refused him, and knew she would be no easy conquest.

"You have been married barely six months!" she pointed out. "You *must* have found Esther agreeable, or you could never have tolerated the union, whether or not your father demanded it!"

He gripped her shoulder so fiercely that she almost cried out.

"You know nothing of my miseries—or my regrets!" he whispered. "Yes, I have endured it for six months! I will endure it no more! She may have my house, my lands, whatsoever she desires, but she will not possess *me* as she wishes to do! You and I will go away—back to Australia, to any place in this world, where she will not find us!"

His urgency puzzled her; she shook her head vehemently.

"You know it cannot be! In time, you would wish you had not acted so hastily and turned away from those things that are rightly yours. This is sheer folly!" she urged. "You were so happy at the thought of coming home when you left Australia!"

"If you cared for me, you would not question me so!" he raged.

She urged him to remember that he owed a duty to his land and his people. He laughed, and told her bluntly that the land was riddled with debt, his people discontented and drifting away to the towns. She listened, troubled, to his urgings, his pleadings and cajolings, to go away with him as soon as possible; but she remained firm, and finally he seized her angrily, pulling her close, smothering her face and lips and neck with hard, violent kisses.

"There!" he cried. "Will THAT not tell you better than my words that I mean what I say? That I will go anywhere, to the ends of the earth, with you!"

"I, also, would have gone as your wife, Richard!" she retorted quietly. "*Never* as your mistress! We must go back to your guests—you will offend them by your absence."

"Let them be offended! They are HER guests, not mine! Say you will come tomorrow? That you will meet me in the little coppice that marks the boundaries of Cousin Philip's land," he begged.

"It is wrong—" she began.

"Why?" he sneered. "Have you succumbed to Philip's charms, so that you can think of nothing else save him?"

"Richard, you sound like a sulky child, not a man!" she said sharply.

"It is because I desire you so much! I *must* see you again! I must talk with you! Tomorrow at three?"

"Very well," she said wearily; she knew that her desire for him matched his for her, but she kept a tight rein upon her feelings, as though she rode a mettlesome horse that required all her wit and skill to master it. Together, they went back to the ballroom; she knew how many eyes noted their entry, how many comments were whispered behind raised fans. She held her head high, although the colour ran in her cheeks as if she had sat in the hot sun. She was aware of the sneer on Philip's mouth, the forbidding look in his eyes; Esther's smile was triumphant; she knew that everyone was curious because of her husband's outrageous behaviour with the woman whose arrival at Russington had caused a great deal of speculation. Some cast-off mistress of Richard's? A pretty little slut of Philip's, kept by him just so long as she amused him? Esther applauded, silently, all they said about Richard; but she resolved to speak to Philip, point out gently the folly of allowing this very dangerous young woman to stay any longer under his roof and protection.

Towards the end of the evening, Taroola asked her hostess:

"Where is Lady Eleanor? I do not see her amongst your guests."

"She preferred to dine alone in her apartments, my dear. I am sure you understand that she does not like to be disturbed from her own little world, in which her son is a child again, and her husband at her side," Esther replied smoothly.

Unexpectedly, however, Taroola saw Eleanor, in the flurry of farewells, the mêlée of departing guests, servants coming and going with wraps, waiting carriages. Philip had gone to enquire into the delay concerning the arrival of their carriage. A hand rested for an instant on Taroola's arm, and she saw Eleanor hovering, uneasy, eyes bright, as though she was ready to take flight.

She drew Taroola back into the shadows, and whispered:

"I have been waiting to see you! You have been kind

to me—but she would not let me come this evening, my dear. She said that I should embarrass the guests by my presence!"

"I am sure she did not mean that!" Taroola protested.

Eleanor nodded.

"I do not know why my husband permits her to stay. She means us harm; so I am entrusting *this* to you. Look after it for me. You must not tell *anyone* you have it, do you understand?" The thin, bony fingers bit with fierce, frantic anxiety into the soft, chilled flesh of Taroola's arm. "You will look after this for me? And not tell anyone? Keep it until I decide what is to be done with it?"

Taroola took the small package, and, to placate the old lady, hid it in the big inside pocket of her velvet cloak, pulling the heavy folds closely around her. "There, you see! It is quite safe with me! I will keep it hidden until you ask for its return!" she said.

"You promise?" Eleanor insisted. "If it is in this house she will find it! But *you* promise to keep it safe for me? And give it only to me?"

"Upon my word of honour," Taroola told her solemnly.

Eleanor sighed with relief; she smiled, and was gone, like a ghost in the shadows. Miss Brandon would take good care of the package, she thought, nodding to herself. When Thomas came home, she would ask him what she should do about it. Perhaps it should be given to Richard when he was old enough to be entrusted with secrets.

Taroola looked at the sealed package; old love letters, perhaps, she thought pityingly; Eleanor seemed afraid of Esther Roxton, and certainly she had no love for her daughter-in-law. Uneasily, Taroola pondered upon the strange things that Eleanor had said, until Philip came back and told her curtly that the coach was ready to take her home.

They sat together in silence, as on the outward journey; she was aware of furious anger in him, and she did not care. She thought only of Richard's anguished kisses, the wildness in his voice when he had begged her to go away with him.

It was very late, and the house was silent, dark, humped against the sky like a sleeping cat. In the hall, candles flickered in their silver candlesticks, ready for them to take to their rooms.

"Do you wish to have a nightcap?" Philip enquired coldly.

"No, thank you. I am very tired," she replied equally cold.

"Not with an evening's strenuous dancing!" he retorted. "Come to the drawing-room; there is something I wish to say."

Astonished, about to refuse, she capitulated; the master of Russington was quite capable of enforcing his request, she knew, and she had no desire to see the servants roused. She knew very well what he was going to say to her.

The remains of the fire still glowed; Philip kicked them into life. A decanter and glasses had been left by his chair, and the small flames winked in the heavy cut crystal. He moved leisurely around the room, as though he had all the time in the world, poking a taper into the heart of the fire, lighting candles in their sconces. His shadow bobbed on the wall, enormous, grotesque, and the moon filled the garden beyond the long windows with pale ghostlight.

The last candle lit, he turned and looked at her, where she stood beside the fire, watching the flames lick the edges of the logs.

"Well, Miss Brandon?" he said sharply.

She looked up, chin tilted, in that infuriatingly independent, unfeminine way that outraged him; women should be meek and small and soft, not proud and aloof, like this one, he thought.

"Yes, Mr. York?" she said defiantly.

"I think you know what I am about to say."

"Perhaps." She came directly to the point. "You are going to remark that I was absent too long from the ballroom this evening, with your cousin."

"I intend to do more than remark upon it!" he retorted violently. "You behaved disgracefully! Your absence with your hostess's husband was an indiscretion, remarked upon by everyone!"

"I did nothing of which I am ashamed!" she cried.

"That, madam, is a matter for your own conscience! Whilst you are under my roof, I am responsible for you!"

"Responsible!" She threw the word at him, her eyes bright and angry. "I am of age, Mr. York! I am aware that I have been compelled to accept your hospitality—reluctantly, as you know—but you will not have to suffer my presence here for very much longer!"

He strode across and confronted her, his anger a tangible thing, like a great gale threatening to blow her from her feet.

"And where, pray, will you go? To Richard? His wife has suffered much on his behalf during their brief marriage, but I fancy even *she* would not tolerate your presence at Roxton! Richard is a spoiled boy, a wilful, indulged child, and she is trying to make a man of him! I will not see you make a mock of her! You came seeking Richard because of idle promises he made you. It would be better had you remained in Australia!"

"I would do nothing to harm Richard!" she cried.

The forlorn note in her voice roused his fury afresh, so that he almost choked on the words.

"You were his mistress at Taroola! Will you give yourself again so easily to him?"

Her hand struck his cheek with lightning speed; he felt the sting of the blow that her palm and fingers dealt him. Enraged, he caught at her hand as it descended; she struggled, but the heavy velvet folds of her cloak hampered her. She brought up her other hand, and he

caught that, too, holding her off. She had dealt him a
blow that made his cheek tingle; but realizing the ease
with which he held her off, she glared at him.

"How *dare* you! I, Richard's mistress? I have *never*
been so!"

"I heard you together!" he retorted implacably. "The
night I stayed at Taroola. I was awakened by a noise;
when I sought to discover its source, I heard the sound
of your voice and his laughter from behind the door of
your room."

She thought back, and her answering voice was full
of bitterness.

"I remember it! Richard came to my room!" Her
cheeks and eyes were brilliant, but her glance did not
falter. "He came no further than the window; I sent
him away! I do not care what you believe, it is the
truth!"

He knew, suddenly, that it was; the anger went out
of him. He saw the glitter of tears in her eyes; *and all
this time,* he thought, *I have believed. . . .*

"Anne," he said softly.

She looked startled; no one ever called her that—her
father had insisted upon 'Taroola.' Her own name
sounded strange on the lips of this man, standing so tall
and proud above her. There was a curious look upon
his face, as though he did not want to take his eyes
from her; but she hated him with a fierce strength that
was only momentarily stayed by sheer surprise, when
he bent his head and caught her close to his heart.

Richard had kissed her; wildly, passionately, as
though to underline the force of his arguments and
state his burning need of her; this man was kissing her
gently, but hungrily, as though he had not known the
extent of his thirst until he touched her; with desire,
but without lust; with all the strength of his being, but
without violence. She felt confused, tormented; quickly
she turned her face away; but he would not let her go,
and, perversely, she was glad. Then, suddenly, he re-
leased her and said quietly:

"I am sorry that I have misjudged you. Tonight's happenings gave me no inkling that I might have been wrong," he added, with sudden jealousy. "What did he want with you for so long? Do you still love him so much that you care not a fig for reputation? Is that it?"

"I—I cannot answer you," she said hurriedly, gathering up her skirts.

With a sob, she turned and ran, wrenching open the door before Philip could reach her. She sped up the shallow, moonlit stairs to the sanctuary of her room; it was so full of pale light that she did not need a candle. She had told Nanny to go on to bed, and not wait to undress her. She was so weary, so exhausted with the night's happenings, that she let her cloak fall to the floor, where it lay like a deep, ink-black pool; then she fell upon the bed, still dressed.

She was asleep when Philip paused at her door. He called her name softly, and she made no answer; he turned the handle and went in. The light from the moon sparkled on her jewels, her dress, her bright, disordered hair. He was shaken with a storm of longing that shocked him; he wished, for an instant, that he was like his Cousin Richard, and could have taken her as she slept there, kissing her protests away when she awoke and felt his hands about her; but he set his mind stubbornly against the idea. He would not have it that way; an unwillingly taken woman was a sad victory and no tribute to his strength or masculinity. He wanted her to come to him freely, though he doubted that she ever would.

CHAPTER SIX

Esther slept very late, for the previous evening had been a strenuous one. She awoke to a room filled with strong summer sunshine, and lay there, contented as a cat. She wondered, idly, where Richard was; riding in the park, with Bessie Lowndes, on his way to London with a curt little note left for her? She neither knew nor cared.

She contemplated, quite dispassionately, the fact that Richard would be hanged on the evidence carefuly hidden in the old Nursery; no fancy lawyers to defend him this time she reflected, no money poured out in his defence. The law did not like to be cheated, so it would punish him all the more righteously. She hated him and despised his weaknesses; she had tolerated him all these months only from expediency. It would not have done to have struck too soon; first, she had let his own reputation build itself up against him, so that others would despise him as she did; Esther was shrewd enough to know life would be easier with amiable neighbours when she lived in the County, as mistress of Roxton Park, after Richard was tried and hanged.

Philip, she thought lazily, would be an easy conquest; but she frowned, suddenly, remembering the girl, and the sunshine was clouded for a moment. Impatiently, she thrust aside the bedclothes, and pulled a wrapper about herself.

When she had dressed and eaten, she went along to the Nursery, and picked up Sebastian; he was in a tantrum and pulled away from her angrily. The young nursemaid looked flustered, for she had spent a gruelling morning with him; but Esther was in too good a humour to be perturbed by the screaming and kicking. She held him close and called him her 'little love' before she went on her leisurely way, pausing often to savour the delight she felt in the vast house, planning all she would do, as mistress. Richard had said he was near penniless; if that was so, it would not matter. He was unaware of the money she owned, carefully hoarded away; a sigh of pure pleasure escaped her lips, as she contemplated her life here; and there was that other glittering prize—Philip.

She decided she would drive over to Russington in

time for afternoon tea and a talk with Philip; and, early tomorrow morning, she would drive into Quinton St. John, to see the local Magistrate, appearing suitably shocked and distressed at the 'evidence' she had 'found' amongst her late father-in-law's papers.

She shook with silent laughter, imagining the Magistrate, kind, fatherly, telling her that she behaved with great courage and honesty in bringing the papers to him.

Philip bit back exasperation when Esther was announced, at teatime. He was in a furious rage that he controlled with immense difficulty, for he had seen Taroola with Richard by a gate in the Little Coppice, as he was riding home from the village. They had not seen him; Richard was holding Taroola's hands, talking urgently to her, whilst she listened with downbent head. Philip had ridden on, seething with anger, and was awaiting Taroola's return when Esther arrived.

She chatted gaily about the previous evening, and remarked that Miss Brandon was a most presentable young woman, before she came, gently, to the point.

"Philip, I speak as a friend, and trust you will take no offence. You must have noticed, as I did, Richard's prolonged absence, with Miss Brandon. I know that he falsely made a promise to marry her, before he left Australia, and I am distressed that he should have behaved so towards her. Because of Richard's indiscretions, you have been forced to shelter Miss Brandon beneath your roof. How long will you keep her, Philip? There is gossip about the situation, you know."

He said shortly:

"I gave her father a promise that I would give her what help or advice she might need, if ever she came to this country. I am obliged to honour that promise."

"She must have relatives, Philip; it is her duty to seek them, *their* duty to shelter her, not *yours!*"

He walked across to the window, and stared out at

the green sweep of parkland, drowsy in the sun.

"I am making efforts to discover the whereabouts of her relatives," he told her.

She sighed with relief.

"I am so thankful." She spread her hands helplessly. "Richard continues to humiliate me with his affairs. Life is not easy for me. Philip."

Her voice was soft; as he turned, she looked pleadingly at him, but he was still thinking of Taroola, and she knew it.

He walked out to her carriage with her; she had not been gone many minutes before Taroola came into the house. Philip was waiting for her; curtly he told her to come to his small study, and her eyebrows rose, her voice was ironic.

"Yesterday, you summoned me to the drawing-room, as though I was a servant or a child to be rebuked; what offence have I committed *today?*"

He made no answer; he turned and walked to the study, and, reluctantly, she followed him. He held the door open for her, and closed it firmly behind her; she looked at him scornfully, seeing the familiar pose by the fireplace: hands behind his back, eyebrows drawn together, face furious and forbidding. She had no idea of the torrent of jealousy she aroused in him; she looked very desirable in a dress of some pale material, her hair worn high on her head, not flowing free as she had worn it when he first saw her; no doubt she thought the upswept hair more decorous for an English household, he thought drily. Her eyes were large and brilliant, and there was colour in her cheeks as though she had been running.

"I saw you not an hour since," he told her. "You were at the gate in the Little Coppice with my cousin."

"That is not your concern!" she flashed at him.

"Have I not told you that what you do in this house is my concern?" he cried furiously.

"I would remind you, Mr. York, that you brought

me here when I was in no state to decide whether or not I wished to enjoy your hospitality!"

"Why, you ungrateful chit!" he said bitterly; she knew it was true, and that she had hurt him once again.

"Tomorrow, I shall leave here, and you will not be troubled with me again!" she cried.

"Tomorrow?" he stared at her in sheer disbelief. "Where will you go?"

"That does not concern you!"

"And Richard? Does he go with you?" Philip demanded curtly.

"No," she replied.

"Ah! No doubt he will join you later! His place is here, at Roxton! Do you wish him to forfeit all he has inherited, knowing that he can never marry you!"

"I have not said that I will enter into a liaison with Richard!" she cried, exasperated; she was exhausted and near to tears. The hour in the coppice had been a stormy one, for she had remained adamant in the face of Richard's pleading, his anger, his final sulky humour in which he had cried out to her that if she did not flee the country with him she would never see him again.

"My promise to your father was that I would give you what help and shelter you needed if ever you came to this country," Philip pointed out.

"I am grateful; but able to manage my own affairs," she said briefly.

"So you have said before!" He was exasperated with her. "I tell you that no woman, even one comfortably placed in life, can hope to fend for herself out in the world! You have no idea what it is like!" He gestured around him. "Here, as at your father's house, you are protected from all that is unpleasant!"

"When I meet unpleasant things, I will do battle with them!" she retorted proudly; and he thought, once again, what an extraordinary woman she was, how unlike most of her sex. It was a difference that infuriated as well as strongly attracted him; she would be a unique woman to have at one's side, he thought. He had known since last night that this was what he desired more than anything in the world. He, Philip York, had never wanted any woman; his feelings for this one were the strongest—and strangest—he had ever known. He was unused to the pretty phrases and sugared endearments of courtship, and his emotions were too tremendous to be pressed into an ordinary mould of words.

He said abruptly:

"I will give you shelter here for the rest of your life; and the protection of my name. I have never had the time or inclination to dote upon a woman, but you are different; and I need a wife. I have no woman to sit at my table, nor to help me with the claims of my tenants; also, I need an heir. These seem to me to be excellent reasons for marriage."

She stared at him in surprise and sheer disbelief.

"Marry you?" She almost choked. "You make it sound like a business transaction!"

"Such was not my intention!" he said formally; he felt helpless. He wanted to take her, shout his love for her, possess her utterly; he wondered how long the torrent could remain dammed within him; yet he was aware that her heart was still held by Richard, and that fact made him angry with her.

"I cannot marry you!" she said. "There is more to a marriage bed than those conditions you name; and any child I bore would be conceived in love!" She met his glance directly, without coyness, and he thought once again that she bore no resemblance to any woman he had ever known; she was as invigorating as the sharp winds that came with autumn, as the hoar frost that chilled the air and stung one's breath.

"Have you reason to suppose that it would *not* be conceived in love?" he demanded. He strode across the room and caught her against him.

"Anne," he said. *"Anne!* I will not call you 'Taroola!' It is an absurd name, without dignity. I want you!

Last night, you knew that! You will be my whole life, here! Do you truly believe that I feel no more than affection for you—that I ask you to marry me merely from expediency? I am not an easy man with words; my actions have always spoken for me!"

Alarmed, she stepped back; she remembered how he had kissed her the previous evening, her confusion of feeling. She put a hand to her head.

"I am sorry!" she said frenziedly. "I—I *cannot* love you as you appear to love me! If I married you, it would be mere gratitude on my part, and in time we might come to hate one another because of that!"

He said bitterly:

"*Richard!* He is the one man in all the world you want? Admit it!"

"Yes!" she cried. "It is true! I have never denied it to you. Have you not considered that if I married *you,* I should be near to *him?*"

"As my wife, you would not seek Richard out nor behave indecorously as you did at Roxton Hall last night!" he retorted.

"And as I am not your wife, nor ever will be, I am free to behave as I choose!" she replied. "You would manacle me, Philip! That I would not endure!"

"Do you prefer the doubtful pleasure of being a man's mistress?" he demanded.

She drew a deep breath; he loved her. It was written, strongly and clearly, in his rugged face.

"Listen to me, Philip," she said, "and then let me go my way. When I was in Australia, my life was lonely. I knew few men. I had never met a man like Richard, though my father distrusted him. Richard talked to me about England, his home there, his life. He spoke little of the crime of which he had been falsely accused. He said no more than that it was robbery."

"It was," Philip said shortly. "An innocent servant carrying jewellery to his master's wife, a woman of considerable wealth and position, staying in the country, and desiring to have certain jewels to wear, was set upon, attacked and robbed, near a small town in Norfolk. He had been delayed and it was getting dark when the attack occurred; someone must have known his movements extremely well. Be that as it may, my cousin Richard was found, some distance away, dishevelled, blood and bruises upon him—the servant had put up a tremendous fight; someone testified that he had seen Richard running from the scene of the crime. The man died later; none of the jewels were ever found, and Richard swore he had been innocent, that *he* had received his injuries when he had been thrown by his horse, on his journey. Richard's father spent a vast amount of money on lawyers, but Richard had kept bad company, he had already been involved in many unsavoury scandals, and was reputed to be an accomplished thief. The witness swore on oath that he had seen Richard running from where the man was found dying. However, Richard protested his innocence to the day he was transported. For a poorer man, it would have been Tyburn, not the convict ship."

"He *was* innocent!" Taroola cried. "You brought a pardon with you! A man confessed!"

"Yes. Matthew Warby. He had been a criminal all his life, and Richard knew him well. When he was dying, he sent for Richard's father and said that he had committed the crime and Richard had not been with him that day. From a distance there was a certain resemblance between the two men."

"Yet you speak as though Richard was still guilty!" she protested, angrily. "Let me finish my tale. I loved Richard. I hoped that, one day, he might work out his time, and be free and we would marry. My father was angry—but I would have married Richard in defiance of him. A pity that Richard ever returned to England to marry a woman he did not love."

"He was not compelled to marry her!" Philip retorted scornfully.

"It was his father's wish, so Richard told me. I think he believed that he would not see me again. That he should honour his father's request. Oh, I do not know *what* he thought, or *why* he chose to forget the promise he made me, but he has entered into a marriage that has brought him only unhappiness!" she cried unhappily.

"He has filled you with idle tales! Esther Roxton has been a good wife to him! She is much more deeply concerned than her husband as to the fate of the farms and land and cottages which he neglects!" Philip retorted.

"Well, I have told you that I shall leave here tomorrow!" she cried unhappily. "It is for Richard's sake that I am going, in case the day should come when I can no longer resist his pleas! If I am not near him, it will be better for us both. How COULD I have wed you, and lived so near to Richard? Do you not understand how deeply I care for his well-being?"

He saw her complete rejection of him; she wanted nothing of him, and he hated himself for desiring her. She was not the first woman to love a rogue, nor would she be the last.

She saw the bitterness in his face and knew herself to be the cause of it. He had not let her finish her story; he had not wanted to hear of the hope with which she had come so impetuously to England, looking no further into the future than a meeting with Richard in which all would be explained and made right. She had not believed the gossip that he was married; the shock of finally discovering the truth had made her more ill than the fever following her drenching in the storm. When she had recovered, she had willed herself to consider Richard no more than a friend, believed that when she removed his ring, she had conquered her feelings for him. She had accepted Esther's invitation to Roxton Hall, thinking that she could meet Richard without emotion; and when she had seen him again, she had known the weakness of her defences against him, as they crumbled around her.

Philip would not have wanted to hear such a tale; nor to have known the depths of her misery, her belief that only by removing herself from Richard's life could she best help him. She thought of Richard's wild talk about a hold Esther had over him; it was nonsense, she thought wearily, a trick to wear down her resistance. Nevertheless, she distrusted Esther, and Eleanor's comments had done nothing to alleviate her fears on that score.

To be near Richard and not to be his wife was unthinkable, to Taroola; that much she had learnt this afternoon in the Little Coppice when she had longed, with all her being, to surrender to Richard's demands to go away with him. Philip's astonishing proposal of marriage had only strengthened her resolve to remove herself from the two cousins.

Philip felt savage fury; if only he could have held her prisoner, he thought, until she saw Richard for the weakling and the coward that he was! It was not in him to coax, cajole, plead his cause, as Richard had done; he was too proud a man.

"As you are determined upon leaving here as soon as possible, there is nothing I can do further," he said icily, "except to tell you that my carriage is at your disposal to take you as far as you wish to go."

Tears filled her eyes; gently, she put a hand on his arm, but he never moved. Only a muscle quivered in his cheek.

"Thank you, Philip. I know that you have been kind, and I must have seemed churlish. I cannot do other than what I believe to be right, though my heart would have me go in another direction altogether to the one I shall take. I wish I could have loved you enough to marry you; but surely you must see how disastrous a union it would be?"

He turned away, and looked at the sun-drenched

lawn where the first curled leaves of autumn spun, like scraps of torn brown paper, in a vagrant breeze.

"There is something you should know," he said. "I have instructed my solicitors to attempt to trace your relatives."

Anger sparkled in her eyes for a moment.

"You should not have done so! Have I not told you that I will have none of them?"

"What crime did they commit that you should be so unyielding in your hatred?" he demanded drily.

"The quarrel was between my mother's and father's family; have you read William Shakespeare's play, 'Romeo and Juliet?' I confess I shed many tears over it, when my father read it, to me; he likened their quarrel to our family quarrel, and my parents suffered much because of the bitterness on both sides. I have no wish to know the people who were the cause of their suffering."

He knew it was useless to comment; he merely asked, in a voice devoid of emotion:

"If you still reject your relatives, are there no friends of your father's, or your mother's, to whom you can go when you leave here?" he asked.

"Please do not be concerned on my behalf," she said evasively.

He turned, angrily.

"*Concerned?*" he cried savagely. "If I could prevent your going, I would use any means at my disposal to do so! It is the knowledge that I *cannot* prevent it that I find so unendurable! You do not know what you are doing! You will attract every knave, trickster, thief and rogue that walk the highway! A young woman, of good countenance, obviously with means, *alone*—oh, you have no conception!" He gestured helplessly. "You are a stubborn, wilful child who should be restrained for your own good!"

He slammed from the room, and left her standing there; she had never felt so alone in all her life. For one wild moment, she considered running away with Richard; the thought tormented, like a gnat. It would be so easy; they would be happy. Ah no! she thought, shaking her head. There would come a day when he remembered Roxton, and the leaves blowing in autumn, the good English countryside, the lands and farms that he despised only as a sign of his own discontent in his marriage. Philip had spoken of him as a profligate, keeping bad company, unscrupulous; Nanny Gaunt had hinted that he enjoyed many women, not all of them wholesome. *I* do NOT care. Taroola thought; he has been young and foolish, but he has not done any of the great wrongs at which they hint. Because he was transported for a crime he did not commit, they have all made a great gale out of a little summer breeze. They have condemned him; oh, I know his faults! He can be a sulky boy, his tongue can be cruel, but he is the first man I have loved, and I will not believe such ill of him!

She remembered the address that she had carefully copied, when she had sorted through her father's belongings, after his death. She went up to her room, thankful that she had not brought a vast amount of luggage with her; nevertheless it seemed a great deal. She folded her muslin dresses and bed slippers, the yellow dress and velvet cloak she had worn the previous evening, packing everything methodically; Nanny Gaunt was away, visiting her sister, until the following afternoon. Best to be gone early in the morning, she decided.

She dined alone with Philip, acutely aware that he watched her, across the polished table top, whilst the candles made points of light in the crystal, and the fire snapped between the logs on the hearth. He watched her, saying little, and their conversation was formal; she wondered, suddenly, what it would be like to be here, always, at this man's table, and knew a moment's sharp, stabbing sadness at the thought of her coming

departure. She would never return again to either Russington Park or to Roxton; for the first time, it disturbed her to think that she would not see Philip again;
she had already set her mind and heart against seeing
Richard. He had told her he would meet her at the
Little Coppice again tomorrow at three, and she realized he would wait in vain for her.

After dinner, they sat in the small drawing-room; for
the last time, Philip thought. A pulse beat in his
temple, and he could not take his eyes from her face.
Taroola stitched at a piece of sewing, and after a while,
she excused herself, saying that her head ached, and
she wished to go to bed. He thought how empty his
house would seem tomorrow and wished that his
flood-tide of feeling had been for anyone except this
woman so defiantly set upon following her own will.

"At least, tell me your destination," he said curtly.

She shook her head.

"So that you or Richard can come seeking me? No,"
she said quietly. "It is better if I consider this time I
have spent here as some part of a book that I have
read, and one that no longer concerns me. For I shall
not come back."

"Would that Richard was worth your foolhardiness!"
Philip said bitterly. "Well, Anne Brandon, I plead with
no woman. If ever you desire to return here, you may
do so. I wish you well."

She hesitated, then went from the room without a
word; he held his longing for her, with difficulty, in an
iron cage of will-power and his face was unreadable.

Philip was up and out early in the morning because
he had no wish to see her leave; he rode far and fast on
his horse before he turned the animal homewards
again; the morning air was cool, and the sun came dif-
fused through delicate mists like muslin drapes that
hung low over the hills. There was dew on the grass
and on the leaves, and the spiders'-webs along the

hedgerows looked like an intricate design of lace hung with minute silver beads. It would be an early winter this year, Philip thought; it was barely September, and Harvest Festival yet to take place in the village church. He would have liked Anne to have seen that; the pumpkins and sheaves of corn, the plaited bread, the brown stone jars of michaelmas daisies, the eggs in their nests of moss, the fruit and vegetable offerings. He had followed his father's custom of donating the Harvest Festival gifts to the almshouses and the poor of the parish. Richard, he knew, exacted the gifts as a due to Roxton Hall, and that was his affair. Anne had never attended such an English festival; he wished that there had been time to show her such things, to have taken her with him when he visited his tenants; how different she would have found an English farm from an Australian sheep station! Now it would never come to pass. Perhaps she would change her mind, go away with Richard, after all, back to Australia, where they would graze their sheep on another station. *Taroola*. He wondered where her father had found such a name, for he liked the sound of Anne; he said it over and over again to himself, as he rode home, and the wind carried her name away.

The servants told him that she had left an hour since. Sprigg, the coachman, said, in response to Philip's enquiry:

"I took her to Quinton St. John, sir."

"Did she say where she would be going from there."

"She said she wanted to get the Mail Coach for London, and asked me if I knew where she should board it; so I showed her, sir."

"I see," Philip said quietly. "Thank you, Sprigg."

CHAPTER SEVEN

If Esther could have torn the old Nursery apart with her bare hands, she would have done so; after the first incredulous surprise and disbelief, she wrenched the saddle from the back of the rocking horse, and thrust, with angry fingers, through everything in the Nursery before she realized that the package had gone.

Stunned, raging with temper, she went to her own room, pacing the floor, trying to think and to still the trembling that shook her. The documents, the precious documents that would rid her forever of Richard! *Someone* had seen her go to the Nursery with Augustus Peach! But who? They had been alone in the room and no one could possibly have been hiding *there,* to see them.

Esther was a methodical woman; as soon as the first fires of savage anger had cooled, she went back to the Nursery, and examined it minutely. She knew all about the lumber room that adjoined it; she picked her way through the accumulated junk, her skirts trailing in the dust of years, and made a thorough search of the cupboard, finally discovering the knot hole.

Who, then? Someone who knew the house well. Richard? She had seen him drive away towards Quinton St. John before she had taken tea with Augustus Peach. One of the servants? It was a possibility; but suddenly Esther sucked in her breath sharply.

Eleanor! She was forever surprising the old lady in strange places. She was sly, secretive, soft-footed; vague and dreamlike though she might seem, she was cunning enough in some ways; but if she had taken the package, what had she done with it? Destroyed it? No, Esther pleaded frantically to herself, *no!*

Grimly, she went along to Eleanor's apartments; the

old lady was alone, sitting by the windows, staring out across the parklands. She looked startled and faintly apprehensive when she saw Esther come into the room and lock the door behind her.

Esther walked slowly across to the high-backed chair, putting her hands on each arm, so that the old lady was penned in. She leant forward, her face white and watchful, her eyes like brilliant green stones.

"Tell me," she said softly, "have you been to the old Nursery of late, Lady Eleanor?"

"No!" Eleanor said quickly and vehemently.

Esther studied the face thoughtfully, seeing the uprush of colour, the frightened way in which the pale blue eyes slid away from her glance.

"You lie!" she said shortly. "You *have* been there, haven't you?"

Eleanor made a feeble attempt at resistance.

"If I have, it is no concern of yours. It is Richard's nursery; I like to go and sit there—" she stopped abruptly, on a sharply indrawn breath, and Esther nodded, her voice quite pleasant.

"Tell me of the last time you were there. No? Then let me help you; it was the day I showed Mr. Peach over the house, was it not?"

Eleanor's lips folded themselves into a stubborn line; Esther brought up her hand, and quite calmly dealt two stinging blows across the old lady's cheek, first one side and then the other. Eleanor began to cry with pain and fright; Esther's strong, thin fingers closed over the bony wrist, as Eleanor tried to put up her hands to shield her face from further assault.

"What did you take from the Nursery?" Esther demanded, still in that deceptively soft voice.

Eleanor shook her head mutinously. Deliberately, Esther struck her again across the cheeks; but Eleanor turned, with an unexpected burst of anger, and thrust her reddened face close to the small, white one with its bright, hard eyes.

"How dare you!" she cried. "I shall tell my husband what you have done!"

"You are an old fool!" Esther said contemptuously. "Your husband has been dead these many months!"

"My son will deal with you!" Eleanor cried piteously.

"Your son!" Esther spat the words. "That cringing weakling? No, madam! No one will deal with *me;* you took a package that I had hidden for safe keeping, from the Nursery. Did I choose to make the contents of that package known, then your son would be hanged. So you must see that it cannot be allowed to remain where someone might find it, and do harm to Richard. Give it to me, Eleanor!" The voice wheedled softly; the hand came up again, but Eleanor cringed away from it, frightened; pain and shock had muddled her already confused mind and she could think only that some harm might befall Richard.

"I do not have the package!" she muttered, turning her face away.

Deliberately, Esther put a hand beneath her chin, and forced the face round to hers.

"Come, Eleanor, I have no time for children's games! I want the package that you have—or must I punish you further, as though you were a disobedient child?"

"I do not have it!" Eleanor cried. "I have told you the truth! I gave it to someone! I knew if it remained in this house, it would not be safe!"

The remark had the ring of truth; Esther leaned closer until Eleanor thought that the eyes would bore through her very skull.

"Who was it?" she asked relentlessly. "Who did you give it to?"

Eleanor shook her head; but the hand came up again, stinging and hurting and making her head ring; she cried out desperately:

"Miss Brandon took the package to keep safe for me!"

"A-a-ah!" Esther exhaled on a long, angry breath. The Brandon girl, still love-sick for Richard! The documents could not have come by greater mishap, she thought bitterly! Then, suddenly, she wondered; a sealed packet, handed to her for safe keeping? It was possible that she would not open it.

She stared down contemptuously at Eleanor.

"Perhaps this will teach you to leave well alone!" she said; she swept from the room, and Eleanor began to cry, shivering violently. When Richard came home, she would tell him *everything* that had happened; he would know exactly what to do. He was clever and sensible, like his father, and he would not allow Esther to hurt her any more.

Eleanor sobbed out her story to Richard as soon as she saw him; he listened, with faint pity for what his mother had endured at Esther's hand, trying to fit the pieces together; and then, when he had the complete picture, sudden hope leapt within him. He made his mother go over the story again and again; he drew every small detail from her. He had seen Esther, moments before, leaving the house, and she had looked both angry and agitated; in fact, he had never seen her in such a taking. He pondered it, biting the tip of his thumb. If Taroola had the papers, he was safe enough; but Taroola had gone from Russington—as soon as he had heard the gossip, he had ridden post-haste to Russington, and Philip had confirmed it. Richard had felt as though the ground had been torn away from under his feet; Taroola *gone!* Lost to him in the maze of London, all hope of persuading her to change her mind and go away with him swept up in the wake of her going. Now, perhaps, it might be a different story, he thought.

"Miss Brandon left this morning, Esther," Philip told her; he looked drawn and pale.

"*Left?*" she cried frantically. "Where has she gone? And why?"

"Her reasons are her own," Philip replied. "As to

where, I know only that Sprigg, who drove her into Quinton St. John, instructed her where she should board the coach to London, in reply to her request. I have no idea where she will go, from London. She may have friends; her relatives she does not wish to see."

"Did she leave anything for me?" Esther asked, with remarkable self-control. "A small packet?"

"No," said Philip briefly; his own wretchedness made him incurious, though Richard had asked him a similar question. He merely thought Esther seemed put out, not her usual, composed self. She bade him good-day, and he walked to the carriage with her; after she had gone, he wondered why she had ridden over in such a fine flurry, but his mind was too concerned with the emptiness of his house to dwell long upon the subject.

To Esther, it had become a matter of great urgency to retrieve the package from Taroola. The weapon, the innocent-looking little packet that could open all doors! She felt a sudden paroxysm of violent hatred towards Eleanor.

She did not know how she was going to find Taroola; London was a big place, and a needle in a haystack could be easier to trace. However, the driver of the coach might provide a clue. He would not return to Quinton St. John until the day after tomorrow; she would question him then. And if that produced nothing, she would tell Augustus Peach that the girl *must* be found.

Richard met Esther in the hall; she tossed her outdoor clothes to the waiting servant, and demanded that tea be sent to her. Richard amended the order to include tea for himself; she looked at him coldly, and walked past him. He saw how she trembled, how white her face, how ugly and vicious her mouth and, for the first time since his wedding-day, he felt light-hearted.

He followed her into the drawing-room; she stood with her back to him, staring out of the window.

"Why, Esther!" he said softly. "It seems you have mislaid something of value, and have been to Russington to seek it. I could have spared you the journey, my dear, had you confided in me! Taroola has gone and taken all her possessions with her, for she has no intention of returning. She did not think to entrust to Philip's care the package that my mother gave her. You dealt too harshly with poor mama, Esther! It was unkind of you! I fancy I know what your precious package contained. Now that you have no whip to goad me, no sword to hang over my head, what will you do? Mama has told me the whole story. My clever little Esther! But not, it seems, clever enough—!"

She turned on him, like a spitting cat, her eyes glowing.

"Be silent!" she commanded savagely. "I am not yet done, Richard! What if the package falls, by some mischance, into other hands? If it is opened, and the contents known, your guilt will be shouted as loudly to the world as though *I* had proclaimed it! Where will you hide *then*—behind your mistress's skirts?" she sneered.

"Taroola will take good care of the package," he said smoothly.

She looked sharply at him, from beneath fine, pale brows, her eyes narrow and cold.

"Have you then told her the contents?" she demanded.

"What if I have? Do you think SHE would shout my guilt—or more likely destroy the papers you have guarded so carefully for so long? Come, you know the answer! *She* would *never* shout my guilt aloud!"

Esther looked haggard and pinched about the nostrils; it had been a clever move on his part, Richard thought jubilantly. A superb stroke to make her think that Taroola knew the truth, and was shielding him.

Esther felt suddenly hopeless. Of what use, she thought bitterly, to pursue Taroola for something she had obviously destroyed?

The servant brought tea, and set the heavy silver tray on the table between Esther and Richard; he went

quietly from the room, closing the big double doors
gently behind him. There was an unnatural stillness
about the two people who remained. Esther sunk her
small white teeth into her lower lip, until a bead of
blood spurted; sick rage, crushing defeat, burning
hatred—she felt every violent emotion that it was possible for a human being to know. She wished Richard's
mother dead and conjured up a mental image of
Richard swinging from the gallows at Tyburn, but it
gave her no satisfaction.

She was defeated; but only temporarily, she reminded herself. The documents had been valuable only because they offered a quick, safe means of disposing of
the husband she loathed; they were a stepping-stone to
plans that had been maturing slowly for a long time. At
least, she thought ironically, the precious documents
had won her the title of Lady Roxton, and for that, if
for no other reason, had proved valuable. And Taroola
had left Russington; no longer need she fear that Philip
might find her attractive, and her presence there very
desirable.

All was *not* lost, she reminded herself firmly; her
gaze rested on Richard, who was still smiling triumphantly. Let him smile; if the documents did not
come into her possession again, she would find other
methods of achieving what she wanted. Less spectacu-
lar, perhaps; the loss of her greatest weapon had been a
bitter setback; in spite of that she would set to do what
she had planned, and she would yet be Philip York's
wife, she reminded herself.

Richard felt as though a great stone that had hung
round his neck had been removed, and in consequence
he was prepared to be nice even to Esther; but as soon
as tea was over, he rode fast into Quinton St. John and
called on Bessie; she looked affronted that he should
come so early, when she was wearing an old print
dress, and her hair was still in rags; he shook his head,
laughing, at the question in her eyes, and tossed a

handful of money at her; he was his old, rakish, devil-may-care self again, as he always was when life went his way.

"I want information, no more. You know all that happens here, Bessie. Who drove the coach out this morning?"

"Jack Taggart," she said promptly, picking up the coins before he changed his mind.

"Ah!" Richard looked pleased; Jack was a great friend of Bessie's. He watched the plump white hands gathering the coins, and thought, again, how pretty they were.

"He will not be back for a day or so yet," Bessie pointed out in her soft West-country drawl.

"I know that. When he returns I want to see him. He took a lady to London this morning."

Bessie nodded.

"The one that's been staying at Russington. *Your* lady, I did hear, come all the way from Australia to marry you."

"Never mind that," he said shortly. "I want to know where Jack Taggart set her down in London, and if she was met, or if she said where she would be going once she left the coach. Find out all you can, Bessie. I'll come back the day after tomorrow."

Taroola, uncomfortably jolted over the poor roads, weary of the long journey in the crowded coach, thought about Richard, and Philip, and all that she had left behind. Once in London, it would be easier to make plans, to decide what she would do, she decided. She supposed she must marry someday; but, no, she thought defiantly, *never,* if it cannot be for love! She thought again of Philip's extraordinary proposal and sighed; her thoughts went back to the night she had driven over to Roxton with him; it was only then that she recalled the package Eleanor had thrust into her hands, as she was leaving. She was dismayed almost to the point of tears; that she should have been so careless as to leave it in the big pocket inside her velvet cloak! She had wanted to say good-bye to the old lady, for she had grown fond of Eleanor; but to do so would have meant a journey to Roxton Park, for she could scarcely have summoned Eleanor to Russington.

She sighed, reflecting that the contents probably only had value in the eyes of the woman who had so urgently pressed them upon her for safe keeping; well, she would return the packet as soon as possible. Exactly how she would do so, she did not know, for she distrusted consigning anything to the mail, which could be a doubtful method of communication. She thought, frowning, of the coachman, who was a local man, from Quinton St. John. No, he might forget or lose the packet, she thought dubiously. She would find some better way, and hope, in the meantime, that poor, vague, muddled Lady Eleanor did not miss the packet. Perhaps she has even forgotten already that she gave it to me, Taroola thought.

She was glad when the long journey was over; London bewildered her. She had not expected it to be so noisy, so dirty, so swarming with people. She looked at a barefoot child in a ragged shawl, a pretty little girl of about ten, holding out a sprig of heather; she fumbled in her reticule, and gave the child some money, and within seconds, she was surrounded by a swarm of thin, dirty, barefoot children, holding out their hands to her.

The driver of the coach shouted at them and cracked his whip, until they scattered; Taroola tucked the sprig of heather into the bodice of her dress, and he 'tchk-tchked' in exasperation, as he watched her.

"Shouldn't encourage 'em, miss," he said reprovingly.

"They were poor," she said defensively. "They had no boots or shoes, and some of them looked like bundles of rags."

"Mebbe so." Jack Taggart was not a hard-hearted

man. "If you're going to stay in London, miss, you'll get used to seeing all kinds, rags and no boots, an' all." He looked curiously at her; he had heard the gossip about Russington and the girl who had come seeking Richard. He knew who she was and he wondered what had happened; Mr. York, he thought—now *there* was a gentleman! A pity she didn't settle for him, though it was said he had no eye for women.

"Where are you making for?" he asked Taroola.

"I—I am going to friends," she said hurriedly.

"In London?" he asked.

"Yes," she replied.

"Well, you'll need a cab," he told her; he called to the boy with him to help the lady with her luggage. The last he saw of her was getting into a cab, as he told Bessie when he returned to Quinton St. John. No, he didn't hear where she asked the driver to take her, he had other things to see about. . . .

Taroola thought London an ugly, sour-smelling place and was tormented by doubts as to the wisdom of her journey, a decision made so precipitately. She had no idea what she would find, what kind of address it was that she was going to, although the driver of the cab seemed to know it. She was ashamed of her sudden desire to cry; she, who had boasted so proudly to Philip York that she could fend for herself was already like a frightened mouse scurrying behind the wainscot! Where was her courage, her pride? She lifted her head, as the cab came to a standstill, and saw with relief that they were in a square of tall houses, with a small green park in the centre, shut in by high iron railings. Most of the houses looked fairly prosperous, she thought with relief, the windows well-draped, an air of decorum about them. Nevertheless, as she stood outside Number Seven, panic surged within her again; she fought it back and pulled the bell-rope, realizing how completely she was placing herself in the hands of a woman she had never seen; a woman who might be dead, she thought, with sudden horror; and here she was, with her luggage, and no idea where she would stay if she found no sanctuary here.

The maid who answered her ring was skinny and freckled and round-eyed; she could not have been much more than fourteen.

"Mrs. Chantry?" Taroola said, her voice high and clear and remarkably steady. "Mrs. Ellen Chantry?"

The maid muttered something and nodded and disappeared; well, at least it appeared that Ellen Chantry lived here, Taroola thought, with immense relief. The maid had left the door half open and the hall was comfortably, if ornately, furnished. In the distance, she could hear the sound of high-pitched feminine laughter, and a hastily-muffled giggle; from somewhere inside the house, an older, more authoritative voice scolded the maid.

"Lallie, will you *never* learn to answer the door properly! You will ask the name and business of the caller, and if the name is known to you, then you will show them into the hall and ask them to wait whilst you see if I am at home. How many times have I told you so? I must see for myself who this young woman is, since *you* have not had the sense to ask her name. What she will think of a servant who scuttles away like a crab wanting to bury itself in the sand, I dare not think. For the price one pays nowadays, for servants, it is monstrous that they should be so dull-witted. . . ."

The grumbling was good-natured, Taroola thought; poor Lallie would make the same mistake next time, receive the same scolding, and pay no attention whatsoever.

Ellen Chantry suddenly filled the doorway; she was not a tall woman, but she was very plump, balanced on ridiculously tiny feet like a teetotum spinning. Her hair and her dress were in the fashion of thirty years ago; her ringlets were fussy, ribbon threaded and quite grey; her face was carefully rouged and powdered, and the eyes, though shrewd, were kind. She wore a quantity of

jewellery that clashed and tinkled softly and not un-
pleasingly, as she moved.

"Well, my dear young lady," she said, with a
vagueness somehow reminiscent of Eleanor Roxton, "I
do not know who you are, for my maid did not think to
ask your name."

Taroola said:

"I am Anne Brandon, James Brandon's daughter.
Taroola my father called me; I believe you were a
friend of his. He spoke of having heard from you,
though not of late years, since he went to Australia."

"*Brandon!* James Brandon! *Never!* Ellen peered at
her disbelievingly, then held the door wide. "My dear
child, come in! *James'* daughter! Incredible. How do I
know that you speak the truth?" she added, with sudden suspicion.

"I have papers that prove I am my father's daughter," Taroola said.

In the hall, Ellen blinked at her, then nodded.

"Yes, you have his chin. Stubborn. And his eyes. I
have not heard from him in twenty years! How is he?"

"He is dead," Taroola said; and the small, lonely
phrase seemed to sum up all the bewilderment and unhappiness she had known since she set foot in England.
The tears came unexpectedly, and she could not stem
them; Ellen coped with brisk, kindly efficiency.

"Lallie, some tea, in my sitting-room. Don't *stand*
there, child, tell them in the kitchen that I want tea sent
in; and have a bed made up in the room that was Miss
Anna's. Some hot water, too, Lallie, and clean towels."

She sent the small maid scurrying, and took Taroola
into a room crowded with every possible knick-knack
and piece of bric-à-brac that ever graced a lady's sitting-room. But it was warm, comfortable and welcom-
ing.

The flood of tears left Taroola exhausted, but calm;
Ellen nodded with satisfaction when they finally
ceased, and said:

"Dry your eyes, now, my dear. To cry, sometimes, is

a most excellent thing, and very good for the complexion. Lallie will show you to your room, and tea will be ready when you have washed."

Taroola said wryly:

"You are most kind to a stranger whom you have never met before."

"I had a great affection for your father," Ellen said. "It was I who helped him to elope with your mother. Now—the sooner you are ready, the sooner we can have tea and I must confess I feel the need for it. This has been an exhausting day."

Taroola caught a glimpse of a couple of young women disappearing through a doorway on the far side of the hall; but she was too tired to wonder overmuch about them. She looked with gratitude at the room to which Lallie showed her, thinking how much less fortunate she might have been had Ellen Chantry been dead or of a less generous disposition. The room was clean, with flower-sprigged drapes and hand-crochetted mats, a big wool rug on the floor, and a pitcher full of steaming, scented water beside a china bowl.

With the grime of travel washed from her face, and her hair brushed, she felt renewed; she went rather shyly to Ellen's sitting-room, and apologized for the trouble she had caused. Ellen brushed her apologies aside and poured tea; there was a dark, rich-looking plum cake, a plate of muffins; Taroola realized that she was hungry.

Ellen watched her eat, and thought, sighing, how attractive she was; not at all like Mary Brandon who had been a delicate little creature, fragile-looking as a piece of porcelain. She wondered why Taroola had come to her; she hoped, anxiously, that the girl was not in trouble; she looked well-bred enough, but one could never tell. Young men were wild, these days, and pretty girls were a responsibility; *she* knew *that,* better than anyone.

There was no point in keeping back any of her story,

Taroola decided; indeed, it would have been churlish to have done so, when she had been shown such kindness and hospitality; Ellen heard her out in silence, her curls bobbing and swinging as she nodded or shook her head, her face reflective, her eyes bright and alert, as though she tested each piece of information for its truth, before she made her own assessment, finally, of the entire situation.

"My poor child! Life has been surly towards you of late, it seems! And affairs of the heart are so distracting!" She made an affected, rather theatrical little gesture with her fingertips in the direction of a point just below her left bosom; a sudden spring of humour welled up in Taroola, making her want to laugh, though she kept a sober face.

"It might have been better had you stayed and married Mr. York; by all accounts, he sounds a gentleman," Ellen said shrewdly.

"But I have no affection for him!" Taroola cried.

"Ah well!" Ellen nodded. "You are like your father. He was an impulsive, warm-hearted man. His father and mine were old friends. In those days, before I was married to Mr. Chantry—a handsome scoundrel who up and took my money and jewels and left me near penniless—we played together, James and I. His father had a long-standing feud with Mary Wilton's father, and the children were forbidden to speak to one another. It was a very old quarrel, something to do with a woman, in the days of their youth; and, of course, James and Mary met and fell in love, and James had this wild notion of going to Australia because he said it was a good, new place with opportunities for any man. Well, it was a strange notion and no mistake—nothing but a country for transporting convicts to, full of black men and women, wild and unfriendly; but James was set on it and Mary would have gone anywhere that he took a fancy to; their parents never forgave the elopement; when James first went to Australia, he had a store in Sydney and not much of a living to be made at it; but his father disinherited him and Mary's father swore she should never set foot inside his house again; but I'd hear from them, once a year, perhaps. They were happy enough, money and parents or no. The last I heard was that your mother had died, soon after you were born." Ellen blinked away the tears. "After that, there was silence. Many's the time I've wondered. . . ."

She smiled brightly at Taroola.

"Why did your father call you by such a strange name? Anne you were christened."

"Yes. My mother chose it; it was the name of a tiny place they stayed at once, near Sydney. My mother liked the sound of it, and my father said if ever his dream of a big sheep station came true, he would call it by the same name." She sighed. "He was certainly not a poor man when he died; but he was a lonely one."

"Ah well, the world's full of trouble," Ellen told her philosophically. "My father lost all his money, soon after I married. Most of what I had, Mr. Chantry took, as I told you. The biggest rogue and the fairest charmer that ever was. But there, I've managed. Boarding young ladies; nothing so grand as a finishing school." she said wistfully. "Tradespeople's daughters, needing a little polish here and there."

The idea amused Taroola; she had a vision of Ellen taking a large mop to a cluster of giggling young women.

"It gives me a living," Ellen said comfortably. "Teaching them to have nice manners, to walk and sit properly, and how to speak to a young man, and write a letter; a young lady comes in twice a week to give drawing and French lessons. Mind you, it isn't always easy, these days, to keep an eye on half a dozen young ladies and see to it that they don't give me the slip to meet a man somewhere. And so untidy, and forever losing things!" Ellen's sigh stated that really her burdens were remarkably light.

Taroola said impulsively:

"Will you accept another boarder? Just until I know what I am going to do? I need no lessons save perhaps dancing lessons, but—" she coloured and added frankly:

"I would not be an encumbrance, Mrs. Chantry. I have more than enough money to pay your fees, I am sure."

"Well, now!" Ellen did not pretend to be coy or embarrassed. "That might suit us both very well, for one of my young ladies has just left. You shall call me Ellen." She looked at Taroola and added, with perfect truth:

"There is little enough I can teach you in the way of manners or grace or deportment, my dear; you have inherited it all from your mother."

CHAPTER EIGHT

The weeks that followed Taroola's departure from Russington were the most bitter of Philip's life; he had never thought of himself as solitary, yet now that she had left, the loneliness of the house was almost more than he could bear. His unhappiness was not lessened by the fact that he knew how much she still loved Richard, and that concern for him had been the prime motive for her departure.

He knew an agony of love and longing that found no relief; something he had never expected to feel for any woman. If only he had kept her prisoner by some means, instead of letting her loose in London, innocent and unsuspecting as she was! But he possessed no authority to keep her at Russington, so he hoarded every memory of her, like a miser with his gold; they had seen little enough of one another, rarely talked to-

gether, and she had declined his invitation to drive with
him when he went to the village, around the estate, or
to visit his farms and cottages. The only invitation she
had accepted with any enthusiasm, he thought bitterly,
was the one to Roxton Park. Well, at least the situation
there seemed to have changed since her departure,
though he found it difficult to understand why Richard
should suddenly seem so cheerful and happy. Esther, as
usual, was quiet and self-contained; she drove over to
see him many times.

He asked after Eleanor.

"I seldom see her these days, Esther," he told
Richard's wife. "She used to enjoy walking in the Park,
and sometimes she would come here to while away half
an hour with me or with Nanny Gaunt."

Esther smoothed down the folds of her skirt, eyes
downcast.

"She seems to have little liking for any kind of ex-
cursion these days, Philip. She prefers to sit alone in
her room. I confess I am troubled about her, for she
seems melancholy. I have tried to interest her in little
Sebastian, for the very old and the very young seem to
me to have some kind of link between them; but she
will not tolerate him near her, and appears to resent
my presence and his."

She smiled wistfully at him. What a sensible woman
Esther was, Philip thought. He thought of Eleanor with
compassion, for he was fond of her. Privately, he felt
he could understand her dislike of Sebastian; a noisy,
spoilt child, he conceded, surprised that Esther, so capable in other ways, should have indulged him to such
an extent that Nanny Gaunt objected bitterly to having
to look after the boy, whenever Esther brought him to
Russington.

Philip made enquiries of Jack Taggart as to
Taroola's destination after she had arrived in London;
and Jack had given him the same answer that Bessie
had given to Richard: that he had not heard the direc-

tion given to the cab driver. All he knew was that she had said she was going to friends. Sometimes, sitting alone at night by the light of the fire and the flickering candles, Philip made wild, impossible promises to himself to search London until he found her, knowing full well the hopelessness of such a task.

Taroola found plenty to do at Ellen's, for which she was thankful; it made the days pass more quickly, and allowed her less time to spend in sad thought. When she was alone, a crowd of memories jostled for attention; she wept bitterly, for a loneliness that had begun when she had said good-bye to Richard at the sheep station in Australia; she recalled, also, that Philip had been kind to her; she remembered their last meal together, and the unexpected passion with which he had kissed her on the night they had returned from Roxton. He had asked her to marry him; how much easier her life would have been could she have accepted his proposal. She thought of Philip's strength, his solitary air; a man with a nature like her own, she thought, and quickly crushed the memory; but it was like crushing a sprig of rosemary between her fingertips, for the perfume remained still, and she wished it was not so. Richard was the man she longed for, wanted, loved with all the passionate intensity of which she was capable. No one could take his place.

She was worried about the packet that she had hidden safely away amongst her possessions; she made several journeys to the coach stage before she was able to locate Jack Taggart, and give him a letter she had written to Lady Eleanor.

Jack looked at her with sharp eyes, remembering that Mr. York, as well as Sir Richard and his wife, had seemed very interested in the whereabouts of this young lady; but when he tried to draw her out, she smiled and shook her head and would say nothing.

He took the letter to Roxton Park; but it was delivered into Esther's hands, not to Eleanor's, for the servant brought it to her stating that the Coach driver had a message from Miss Brandon to Lady Eleanor; but as Lady Eleanor was in her bed with a severe chill, he had thought it only right to bring it to Lady Esther.

"Thank you, Tewson," Esther said agreeably. "You did well to bring it to me."

She had no compunction about breaking the small seals; astonished, she read the letter. So the damning evidence against Richard was still in existence! Miss Brandon, it seemed, had no desire to deliver the package personally; if Lady Eleanor would write her, she would call at the coach stage in one week's time to collect instructions as to how she should deal with the package.

Esther could have shouted aloud with joy. Once again, Richard had lied and Taroola did NOT know what the package contained! She thought of the vain enquiries that Augustus Peach had made on her behalf. Thoughtfully, she tapped her chin with the back of her quill, before she began to write the neat little note, stating with regret that she was not well enough to travel to London, but most anxious to have her package, and would ask her daughter-in-law to collect it, one week after Miss Brandon had received this letter. She signed it 'Eleanor.' She doubted very much that Taroola had ever seen the old lady's handwriting.

Esther sat back in her chair, smiling, thinking of the woman who lay ill upstairs, nursed by any of the servants who could be spared for a few hours. It was her own fault entirely that she was ill, Esther thought righteously; several times she had been found wandering in the park, at night, her thin slippers and the hem of her gown soaked. Once she had walked over to Russington, where Philip had found her in a state of collapse and brought her home; she seemed to be more vague, more foolish, than ever. Esther made excellent capital of the fact to Philip, confessing herself worried, and posing as a devoted nurse. Richard was not himself, either, as she pointed out to Philip; one or two strange turns that had puzzled the physician, a weakness and nausea that troubled her greatly. . . .

So she had basked in the warmth of Philip's quiet sympathy; and now—this! She read the letter through, sealed it and gave instructions concerning it. Victory was almost hers, but she was impatient; tired of waiting to be rid of Richard, to enter into possession of Roxton Park and lands, to be entirely her own mistress, and turn her eyes toward Philip.

She thought it would be a simple matter, with the sending of the letter; and it might well have been, but for the fact that Jack Taggart was as big a gossip as any old woman; he retailed the whole episode to Bessie.

Bessie was waiting for Richard, a couple of days later, when he arrived at the house in the little street at Quinton St. John.

"Got a piece of news for you, I have," she boasted. "Nay, I'll not tell you now, but after. . . .

She they made love, and afterwards when he lay beside her in the tumbled bed, she recounted the piece of news that Jack had told her; Richard listened carefully and made Bessie go over the story twice.

"When is Jack Taggart taking the coach to London again?" he demanded.

"Day after tomorrow," Bessie told him.

"I shall be on the coach," he told her calmly. . . .

Richard told Esther only that he would be away for a few days; she shrugged, indifferent; in one week's time, the Roxton coach would take her to London for her rendezvous with Anne Brandon, and the safe delivery of the precious packet. Nothing else mattered to her.

Richard spent most of the long, uncomfortable journey going over in his mind the tale that Bessie had recounted. He had discreetly questioned the servants at Roxton, and Tewson had admitted handing the letter for Lady Eleanor to Lady Esther. Richard had then questioned his mother, who, in spite of the wretched state that she was in, had emphatically insisted that she had not received a letter. He would have given a great deal to know what was in the reply that was in Jack Taggart's safe keeping, Richard reflected; though he knew better than to bribe him to hand it over, for Jack was a man who was proud of his principles; but what mattered most was that the letter would lead him to Taroola who would give him the package that his mother had entrusted to her.

It was a pale, sunless afternoon, fierce with a bitter cold when he reached London; stiff and cramped, he stepped thankfully from the coach, reflecting that he would have travelled a deal more comfortably in the Roxton carriage.

He saw Taroola, before she saw him; she was warmly wrapped in a cloak of some rich, dark material, the hood thrown back to show the paleness of her face, the sheen of her russet hair. He thought she looked thinner, but that fact accented her loveliness and he felt a leap of desire in his pulses for her, cursing the folly that had led him to leave Australia in such haste, when today he might have been married to her, and a good deal better off.

When he stepped from the shadows, and confronted her, she looked, at first, as though she would run away; her eyes widened, and the colour came and went in her cheeks. He was the last person she had expected to see.

"Richard!" she whispered.

He caught hold of her hands.

"You did not expect me!" he said softly and triumphantly. "You fled me, but I have found you!"

"How did you find me?" she whispered.

He told her the story of the letter that Jack Taggart had delivered into Esther's hands; she listened gravely, her eyes wide and troubled. He told her that the coach driver had a reply for her; she looked beyond Richard to Jack, muffled in his great, caped coat, stamping his feet against the bitter chill, the horses snorting, their breath making white plumes on the air.

"Go!" Richard urged. "Ask Taggart if he does not have a letter for you! I should give a deal to know the contents. You *will* tell me, Taroola?"

"What is the importance of this package?" she demanded.

"Later, I will tell you," he promised. He pulled her close to him, in the shadows, his lips lingering against her hair for a moment, until she pulled sharply away, pain in her heart and her voice.

"Better you had not come, Richard! I was learning to forget!" she cried desolately.

"With whom do you stay in London?" he wanted to know.

"That I shall not say; I would not have you or Philip seek me out!"

"Philip?" he said, with a sneer.

"Yes. Because he believes that he should honour the promise made to my father," she replied quietly.

He watched her walk across to Taggart, who gave her the letter from his big leather satchel; he thought, exasperated, of the Roxton town house, in a fashionable part of London, closed now save for an elderly caretaker, the servants dismissed, because he could no longer afford to maintain the place. It was a great bone of contention with Esther, who liked the idea of having a house in London, in which to entertain; she complained bitterly about the near-poverty in which they lived at Roxton.

Taroola came back, holding the letter; Richard glanced at the handwriting, and said contemptuously:

"*Esther's!* Come, we will find a cab, and I shall take you to an eating-house I know where we may have a little privacy!"

She protested that she could not stay away too long; the place to which he took her was fashionable and opulent, with a great deal of red plush, ornate gilt mirrors, marble, and velvet drapes. He managed to obtain a private room; a fire was lighted, and the food brought to them; only then did Taroola open the letter and read the contents. Silently, she passed it across to Richard. He read it through, and nodded curtly.

"Esther has done this. The letter that you sent never reached my mother!"

"I shall not hand the package to anyone save your mother," she replied stubbornly.

"Better still, destroy the package," he said eagerly. "Do this for me, my love."

"You must tell me why, Richard. I believed it to contain personal papers which your mother treasures. Perhaps some old love letters. . . ."

His laughter was derisive.

"Would that you were right! My mother *found* the package; Esther had hidden it, in the old Nursery. It was brought by Mr. Peach, the lawyer, to Esther."

"What is in it, Richard?" she insisted.

He stared moodily into the heart of the fire.

"It contains evidence enough to hang me at Tyburn!" he burst out suddenly, "and to damn my father as a rogue! There! Have I not told you enough? This evidence came into Esther's hands by means which I alone know. Esther came to me, and demanded that I marry her, as the price of withholding the evidence contained in the package; she promised to hand it over to me on our wedding night, but she withheld it then, and laughed in my face when I reminded her of our bargain! That is the truth! I would not have married her had I not been as truly hunted as a deer fleeing a pack of hounds and faced with being torn to pieces by them or leaping to its death over a clifftop. If you have any affection for me, Taroola, any feeling in your heart, I beg you to destroy what the packet holds that I may breathe freely again, and walk without fear!"

It was one of the most impassioned speeches of his life; Taroola stared at him incredulously.

"It is an extraordinary tale!" she murmured.

"True, nevertheless," he replied; and she knew he was not lying.

"Richard." Her voice was quiet. "One thing I beg you to tell me; this evidence you speak of; are you, then, guilty of the crime for which you were pardoned?"

There was a long silence; he said nothing, but when he lifted his head, his face was haggard, and his eyes answered her in the affirmative. She felt suddenly very tired, defeated, and bitterly disillusioned. She did not want to ask more questions, to know more; it was enough to remember that Richard, on whom her heart had been set steadfastly for so long, lived a lie; that he had not told her the truth when he had said his father wished him to marry Esther.

"I will destroy the package," she said, finally.

He came across the room, and caught her arms pulling her close to her, smothering her face with kisses beneath which she remained immovable, unable to be stirred to any kind of feeling; in his relief and jubilation he did not notice that fact.

"My sweet!" he murmured, against her cheek. "My dearest love! Esther is nothing to me except a hindrance to the happiness I seek with you! She was determined upon being mistress of Roxton, and thus she cheated me. But it will not always be so, my darling!" His voice rose, on a note of optimism; relief made him light-headed, as well as light-hearted. At this moment, nothing seemed impossible to him.

"I swear that Esther shall not have her way!" he boasted. "Mistress of Roxton she may be now, but, my beloved, it shall all be changed. . . ." He murmured endearments against her hair, his hands sliding around her waist, a question in his eyes, to which she shook her head sharply, though the blood pounded through her temples.

"Please!" he entreated. "This room is ours for the night if I so choose. . . ."

"No, Richard! We may *not* choose!" she protested; and he let her go reluctantly.

He was a child, she thought suddenly, a small child with a tin trumpet which he blew loudly, making a great deal of noise that signified nothing at all. She knew a sadness like nothing she had ever known; she had believed so passionately in Richard's innocence, and he seemed not to care at all how the knowledge of his guilt dismayed and shocked her; he wanted only to possess her, careless of his honour, his responsibilities, his wife.

It was late when she reached Ellen's house; she walked slowly, dragging her footsteps wearily as though the effort of walking was almost too much. Ellen, who had been waiting up for her, came into the hall and said testily:

"I have been worried for your safety, child."

"You have been a long time out, and in this bitter weather, too."

Taroola smiled, with an effort, at the kindly, plump little woman who peered short-sightedly at her; she let her cloak slide from her shoulders, and said simply:

"I met a friend; we dined, and talked together."

"A young man, I'll be bound!" Ellen said sharply.

Taroola made no reply; Ellen sniffed, disappointed, and said:

"You look as though you need a hot toddy; come to the fireside and warm yourself. . . ."

Much later, Taroola went to her room, pleading weariness in the face of Ellen's desire to sit and gossip; she took the packet from her velvet cloak, and held it in her hands for a moment. The power of life and death, she thought, shivering; as though it seared her

fingers, she dropped it in the grate, and picked up a taper, which she put to the candle flame with unsteady
hands; then she knelt, and set fire to the packet.

It burned quickly, flaring briefly into a pyramid of
flame that warmed her for an instant, and made the
room glow rosily for the same short space of time.
Then the flames dipped, flickered, and died, leaving
only a small heap of grey ash.

Taroola undressed and crept into the high bed
beneath the coverlet, feeling the tears burn hotly
against her heavy lids. The sense of loss, the shock of
Richard's arrival, the realization that he was an irresponsible boy, not a man, saddened her beyond belief.
There was no rest, anywhere, she thought; no haven,
no hope of happiness. Here, at Ellen's, she had found a
measure of peace, though she had little in common
with the giggling young ladies whom Ellen coaxed and
bullied gently into some semblance of elegance; Ellen
was kind, asked few questions, and Taroola was grateful, not looking beyond each day as it came. At this
moment, she felt she did not care if there were no more
days to come, for her. Richard was safe; for that, she
should be thankful, she reflected ironically.

Richard felt a heady sense of triumph; Taroola had
given him her promise and he knew that she would not
fail him. He spent two days in London, frequenting his
old haunts, spending money lavishly, enjoying himself
with women who were only different from Bessie
Lowndes in that their surroundings were more opulent.
On the third day he went home to Roxton; Taroola
had refused to yield up her address, or to see him, but
that fact did not worry him overmuch. Later, he
thought, he would get in touch with her again, when
Esther was no longer at Roxton Park. For he would
make life such torment for Esther, he told himself, that
she would go, and he would be left in peace to enjoy
his father's inheritance.

He went straight to Esther on his return; she sitting in the small drawing-room, the picture of tranquillity, stitching at a sampler, having just returned from a ride in the park with Sebastian at her side. It was her favourite pastime; it brought home to her the grandeur of her position, the fact that she was Lady Roxton, and she savoured it blissfully.

She looked with contempt at Richard lounging in the doorway.

"Well?" she said coldly. "Does it give you pleasure to humiliate your wife by staying out of the house for three days, without the courtesy of stating where you are going?"

He sauntered, smiling, into the room.

"It gives me the greatest pleasure, madam," he said, laughing softly.

She set her lips in a thin line; her eyes were cold, but wary. He was in too good a mood for her liking.

"I have been to London," he told her, watching her face.

"Yes?" She did not look up from the sampler she was stitching.

"I have seen Taroola." Her hand was still only for a moment, then the fingers moved rhythmically again. "I have seen, also, the letter that you sent to her, my dear. I questioned the servants before I went; and you should have remembered, also, that Jack Taggart loves to gossip. So I knew that the letter sent to my mother never reached her; and having seen your reply to that letter, the matter was simple enough; I instructed Taroola to destroy the package that she possessed—and this she has done."

The needle went to and fro; if Esther's hand trembled, Richard never saw the flicker of a movement. She did not even look up.

"Are you sure she has destroyed it?" she asked coolly. "Or will she not, perhaps, keep it for her own ends?"

"Not Taroola!" His voice rose in a joyous shout of

triumph. "She gave her promise! Already it is a heap of ashes. Think, Esther! The weapon that has been yours for so long can never be used again! You have no more power over me! *None,* do you hear?" He bent forward and snapped his fingers in her face, his hatred like a naked flame burning in his eyes. Her own eyes were as cold as glass, as green as emeralds.

"I am still Lady Roxton," she reminded him. "My little package of papers bought me *that,* Richard; a title, the fact of being mistress of this house."

"And how long will you keep all that?"

"I do not know what you mean?"

He laughed and said nothing; let her be afraid, he thought scornfully! Let her wonder what schemes he hatched in his mind. Anything could happen, any kind of accident befall her; he felt a rich satisfaction in knowing that she must feel afraid, defenceless as she was now. Lady Roxton indeed!

He bent forward suddenly, seized the heavy, pale ringlets on her neck and dragged them downwards so that her face was forced upwards to meet his; with his other hand, he tore savagely at the material of her dress, ripping it open to the waist; she twisted from him, opening her mouth to scream, but, quick as lightning, he covered her lips with his hand.

"How I hate you!" he whispered. "How I have hated you since our wedding night!"

She wrenched free.

"Because you could not have your way!" she spat at him venomously. "The thought of bearing YOU another child, filled me with loathing! And you will NEVER turn me from Roxton Park, Richard! Remember that!"

He laughed, still forcing her head back with his fierce hold on her hair.

"I could take you now, had I mind to! Tumble you on the floor, like any girl in a haystack, and bruise that soft white flesh of yours! But I have no appetite for you, after all! I am free, Esther, free of you forever."

"The day will yet come when you will wish that your father had never bought you a pardon!" she sobbed furiously.

He struck her hard across the face, and let her go so abruptly that her head jerked forward.

"The one man who could have saved you, my dear, is dead!" he jeered.

He went as slowly from the room as though he had all day; he looked carefree and unconcerned. Esther sat in the thin, fading sunlight of the winter afternoon, her hair falling about her face; with trembling fingers, she tried to hold the ripped bodice across her breast. Her head ached from the blow he had dealt her, and a bright bead of blood spurted from one finger, where she had dug in her embroidery needle, in her tremendous effort to reveal nothing of her feelings to Richard. Unlike his hot rage, her own hatred was as cold as death, the more deadly because it was confined within the limits of what she knew she could do; had she not learned, early in life, that if one plan of action failed, there were always others? She lifted her head, breathing deeply. Richard had signed his own death warrant twice over; once by the way he had used her; and, secondly, because she wanted, more than anything in the world, to be Philip's wife, and was determined that nothing should stop her from achieving her one ambition.

When she went to Richard's room, some time later, he was asleep, sprawled on his back on the bed, mouth open, his breathing heavy; he had not even troubled to remove his boots, and the rumpled counterpane was soiled. She looked down at him, and smiled; the throbbing bruise on her cheek was excellent testimony in the eyes of the servants and her friends, as to Richard's cruelty. Looking down at him, she felt almost sorry for him.

She found his manservant, and instructed him to see

the Master of Roxton Park into bed.

"He is tired from his journeying," she explained smoothly; knowing very well that the bruise was noted as much as the inflexion in her voice.

Esther ordered soup to be heated, and a tray of food to be prepared; outside Richard's door, she took it from the servant, and placed it on a small table; then she summoned Richard's manservant from the room.

"He needs food," she said. "See he takes the hot soup, at least, before he sleeps again."

She watched the tray being carried into the room; there had been indignation as well as sympathy on the servant's face. With downbent head she walked the long corridor, and stood looking out of the big window at the smooth, rolling parklands, the bare trees pencilled against the sky, the distant farms and cottages tucked cosily in the green arms of the hills. Perhaps, after all, she thought, this would be a better way than the denouement she had once planned.

"He struck you," Philip said gently. "Is that not so, Esther? Admit it—that is how you came by the bruise?"

Her eyes filled with tears.

"Yes," she said. "He had been away for three days, and I ventured to enquire as to his whereabouts. I had no knowledge that he planned a journey. He told me he had been in London with Miss Brandon."

Sudden pain contracted Philip's heart, so that he felt as though life was being squeezed from it; so Taroola had lied, pretending to remove herself from Richard for his own welfare, when her sole reason for going to London had obviously been to conduct an affair with him, away from the eyes of his wife and friends.

"I questioned him about Miss Brandon; he was angry, and—" she shrugged. "I am less concerned with his conduct to me, than his health. Once or twice, recently, as you know, he has had mild attacks of a strange weakness and sickness. This morning, he awoke complaining of pain and he vomited. He has refused the physician, and will have no one near him. He has taken a little gruel, that is all. It is the manner in which he lives, Philip." She gestured delicately. "The stench, the dirt, the impure water and food." And the women he keeps company with, her silence added eloquently.

Philip frowned.

"If he is ill, then you must take it upon yourself to call the Physician, Esther," he told her.

She sighed.

"I know; but I have no mind to cross him, for he is so easily vexed, so given to violent tempers which he seems unable to control. His mother has made a little progress, for which I am thankful; she is up and about, and I persuaded her to take a bowl of gruel to Richard, thinking he might accept it more readily from her—which, to tell the truth, he did." She smiled tremulously. "You are kind, Philip, to give such a ready ear to my troubles."

"Whatever I can do to help you bear them, I will," he said formally.

She looked at him with a hunger that would have astonished him had he been aware of it; oh that Philip desired her as once Richard had desired her, long ago, when Sebastian was conceived! It was not yet time, Esther consoled herself; but she fretted at the need for caution, impatient to give herself completely to him.

Some days later, Philip stood at his study window, looking at the wintry landscape; the news from Roxton was disquieting. It was almost a week since Esther had visited him, but she had sent word that Richard seemed to be recovering from his bout of fever; and then, this morning, he had received an unexpected visit from a wild-eyed Eleanor, untidily muffled into a great many wraps against the bitter cold, who had told him that

Richard was very ill. Philip had calmed Eleanor and eventually driven her home; she had said strange things that puzzled him; how Esther kept Richard prisoner, how there had been a package hidden in the old Nursery that Esther wanted, and that she, Eleanor, had given to Miss Brandon. He could not make head nor tail of it, and thought it to be the vague wanderings of a confused mind.

Esther had met him at Roxton; there had been a hue and cry when it had been discovered that the old lady was missing. Thankfully, she had hurried Eleanor away in the care of one of the servants, and then confessed to Philip that she was sorely troubled over Richard, who seemed to have suffered a relapse. Philip had asked to see him.

"He is sleeping, now," she said. "For Dr. Lacey gave him a sedative. Come quietly, then, so as not to disturb him."

Philip had stood by Richard's bed, looking down at his sleeping cousin, whose face seemed thin and pinched. Small beads of perspiration stood out on his forehead and a muscle in his cheek twitched as he slept.

"Should you not consult a London Physician?" Philip asked. "It could be arranged, surely?"

Esther nodded, biting her lip; she looked pale and composed.

"I am greatly disturbed about his condition, Philip," she said quietly. "I do not know what ails him, and Dr. Lacey confesses that he, too, is baffled."

Driving home, Philip reflected that Esther had assumed complete command at Roxton, with a quiet air of authority; it was fortunate that Richard was blessed with so sensible a wife, he reasoned. He frowned over Eleanor's remarks, once again, making no sense of them; the old lady must be a sore trial to Esther, harassed as she was by Richard's illness.

In a few weeks it would be Christmas; Philip considered the fact with little enthusiasm; an extra day's pay for his tenants, that had been his father's custom. The big party for them, the holly boughs and garlands that Nanny Gaunt insisted upon as an essential part of the Christmas scene. The Church decked with greenery, and the Carol Singers outside his front door in a wide semi-circle, the huge log blazing on the hearth. Perhaps it would snow, and the hills and valleys would look beautiful, drifted over with quilts of white; but he had no heart for any of it; the house seemed lonely. He was bitter, and the core of his bitterness was the fact that Richard had been with Taroola for three days in London. He must know, then, where and how she was living, Philip reflected.

The following day, Esther sent word that Richard was slightly better; the next day again, she said he was much improved. So Philip rode over, and Esther, meeting him, was all smiles.

"I do not think we shall need the Physician from London, after all!" she said happily. "The fever has left Richard, and though he is weak, he is much more his old self. Sit with him for an hour, though you must not talk too much, for that will overtax his strength. I am longing for a little fresh air, Philip."

Richard lay back against his pillows, looking white and exhausted; his eyes were bright and restless, and as soon as the door had closed behind his cousin, he whispered urgently:

"She wants to be rid of me, Philip! She will destroy me, if she can!"

Philip looked at him, and frowned.

"Esther said that the fever had left you! I fear she was wrong!" he said.

"No. I speak the truth!" Richard retorted; and he was seized by a violent bout of shivering. "Esther is a mad woman, bent upon destruction—and power for herself and the child!"

Philip was appalled; his cousin was deranged, he

thought. It was apparent in the wildness of his eyes and his speech. Esther knew it, and was trying to hide the fact from everyone, even from herself, he thought.

He calmed Richard, as best he could; but his cousin brushed aside his words angrily.

"You think I am mad, Philip! I tell you, it is the truth! I do not know what it is she does, but she has set her mind upon destroying me, and she is achieving her purpose. I am too weak to fight her!"

Richard lay back, overcome by a fresh wave of nausea; he was trying to remember something that Bessie had once said; but it eluded him, lost in the mists of sudden pain that made him draw up his limbs in agony.

CHAPTER NINE

Riding home, Philip shook his head over his cousin's fantastic outburst. Was there some strain of madness, passed from mother to son, he wondered uneasily? The accusations and wild outburst that Richard had made against his wife troubled him greatly.

Within a few days, Richard was up and about again, although he was very listless; Esther's concern for him, in front of the servants or visitors, infuriated him. In private, he accused her of trying to kill him; the green eyes opened wide, her voice was shocked and surprised.

"*I* try to kill *you*, Richard! Your talk is madness! Dr. Lacey is convinced that your illness is the result of the wild life you have led, and some disease that you contracted whilst in London."

"He is wrong, and you know it! What are you doing to me, Esther? What do you put in the food I eat?"

She stared at him.

"In God's name! Now I *know* you are mad! The food is prepared in the kitchens, your mother brings it to you! *I* have no hand in it!" she cried, sweeping angrily from the room, her head held high.

He put a hand to his throbbing temples; he felt sick, disinclined to eat or drink, for it was after food and drink that the pain cut deep within him, twisting and turning as though a knife traced out a pattern in his stomach. Still, there was something he tried to remember; something that eluded him; he could not think what it was. He felt an urgent desire to get out of the house, though weakness held him prisoner.

He touched nothing that day, although Esther sat calmly at the dining table, eating and drinking without ill-effect, it seemed. She laughed at him, taunting him lightly for his nonsense and saying that all the servants believed him to be out of his mind, and was not the fact that she ate freely of the same food that was served to him proof enough of his folly?

However, he stubbornly set his face against food, though he felt weak. He would drive into Quinton St. John, to the Inn, and eat something there, he decided.

His mother came to him, as he was preparing to leave the house; it struck him for the first time that she looked thin and gaunt, her eyes more vague and restless than ever.

"You are not going away, Richard?" she fretted. "Your father will be home, soon, and will expect to find you here."

"Dammit!" he cried, in sudden rage, "can you not understand he is dead? That he lies in the vault, in the cemetery at Quinton St. John, and has been there these many months! He will not come back *here!* Oh God!" he groaned and shivered, putting a hand to his head. "Would that he had never sent Philip to Australia with a pardon!" he muttered. "Then I should not be in this sorry state!"

His mother looked at him, uncomprehending, pulling

her shawl close about her with one hand, and putting
the other hand timidly on his arm. She looked
unkempt, her hair hanging about her face; Esther had
dismissed the maid who had looked after her for years,
insisting that Hawkins could attend to her needs; but
Hawkins, of the hard eyes and rough hands, scarcely
ever bothered with her, and then with ill-concealed impatience.

"Your father will come home," she promised va-
cantly. "Then all will be well again."

Impatiently, Richard shook off her hand. He could
not stand the confining walls of the house much longer.
Esther had gone out in the big carriage with Sebastian,
so he ordered the smaller one to take him into the
town. Once at the Inn, he ate and drank, and though
he still felt weak, the food and drink seemed to fortify
him. On an impulse, he decided to visit Bessie. He had
not the strength to go to bed with her, but the need to
talk to someone was so strong that he made his way to
her and knocked upon the door of her house.

She answered his knock, with a look of surprise.

"Well, I never!" She held the door wide. "I did hear
you was ill."

"So I have been. Bessie, my wife wants to be rid of
me! She is trying to poison me!"

"Oh, what nonsense!" She tchk-tchked softly. "You
have had a fever, and it has not left your mind. I have
heard what things you have been saying about her!
Come with me, then! I can cure you!" She chuckled at
her own joke, gently tugging at his jacket, urgency in
her fingers and anticipation in her eyes; she enjoyed
Richard, who was as rough and earthy as she was.

With a sigh, he submitted to her ministrations; but
he was still weak and disappointed her, as he had
known he would; he lay on his back in the small, stuffy
bedroom, staring moodily at the ceiling, trying to recall
what it was she had once said to him that he should
remember now.

Bessie listened in silence to a sudden, vehement outburst against Esther. Finally, she said frankly:

"I confess I have no liking for her ladyship. Ofttimes I have seen her shopping in the town, and high and mighty airs she gives herself, indeed. Not that we're good enough these days, for her purchases!" Bessie tossed her head. "She goes further afield. My cousin saw her in Yarncross, not two days since, coming from the Apothecary's; and once in Woolchester. Ah well, 'tis her affair. . . ."

He was half asleep; Bessie roused him with a sharp dig in the ribs.

"Get on with you, now! Here, I'll help you to dress. Proper weak you are, tonight," she said, disgruntled. "That'll teach you to stay at home instead of jaunting up in London town!" She laughed at her own joke, but her laughter grated on him, and he suddenly wanted to be gone.

Esther was waiting for him when he returned.

"I was worried about you, Richard," she said blandly. "For you have been too ill to be out, and you will take further chill from the night air."

He looked at her with contempt, and stalked past her; he felt deathly tired. Her green eyes glowed like lamps and her smile was kind.

Richard's recovery was short-lived; within a week he was again ill, more severely than ever; a distracted Esther sought comfort from Philip, saying that she, personally, would undertake the journey to London to seek a suitable physician for her husband as soon as possible; but she could not leave him until he was a little better, for he needed her at his side during his bouts of delirium.

Philip was greatly troubled; he stood, on the afternoon of Esther's last visit, looking at the heavy sky from which a few snowflakes came feathering lightly; he thought, suddenly, of an old legend his mother had told him, of the snow goose flying south, too late, letting some of her feathers fall as she rode the winter sky. It was a pretty tale; he imagined himself telling it to Anne as they sat by the fire, safe from the wintry rage of a dark night; and he put the thought, determinedly, from him.

He was surprised to see a carriage turn in at the gates; the lodge keeper came out and spoke to the driver, in his huge caped coat and hat, nodded, and directed the coach along the drive. Philip wondered about the identity of his visitors, knowing himself to be poor company and in no mood for a social call.

A manservant came to him, a few moments later.

"A lady and gentleman to see you, sir. Sir Jessel and Lady Minton, with reference to your enquiry concerning Miss Brandon. . . ."

Philip discovered that he was, after all, in the mood for a social call; very much so.

"Take their wraps and have them shown in," he ordered. "Bring tea, quickly; and have fresh logs put on the fire, for they will be cold. . . . Stay, I will conduct them both here myself. . . ."

The servants blinked in bewilderment, as Philip walked swiftly past him.

The man who handed his and his wife's wraps to the servant was tall, distinguished-looking, with thick grey hair, and piercing blue eyes; his mouth was disciplined, but not stern, and there was an air of strength and honesty about him. His wife was a small woman, barely touching his shoulder, with a sweet, placid face, and warm, russet-coloured hair, so that Philip knew at once she was a relation of Anne's. It was she who said, impulsively:

"Your lawyers wrote us, Mr. York, concerning my niece! Her mother and I were sisters, though I never saw my niece. . . ."

"My dear, we should introduce ourselves properly to Mr. York!" her husband said, with good-humoured reproof. She bit her lip and looked up at him ruefully; clearly, there was a great deal of affection between them.

"I think we have much to talk about," Philip said quietly. "On such a cold day, conversation is best conducted over a tea table, by a blazing fire."

He took them to his study; he felt a flicker of excitement in his pulses. Here at last was a link with the woman he loved. Even though she loved Richard, and had fled his house for that reason, he would never cease to love *her*, Philip reflected. He had tried to hate what she had done, the days and nights spent in London, with Richard; he had imagined her, in Richard's arms, caressed, loved by him, and the thought had been torment; but his own feelings for her burnt as fiercely as ever.

The introductions were brief.

"My wife," Sir Jessel Minton explained precisely, "is, as she has told you, the younger sister of Mary Wilton, who married James Brandon, eloping because of the feud between her family and the Brandons." Sir Jessel sighed. "An old quarrel, and a foolish one, Mr. York; over a woman. There are many reasons why men should fall out with one another, but a quarrel over a woman—particularly one of doubtful reputation, as was the case—is sheer folly. The quarrel between the Brandons and the Wiltons seemed to grow with age; but old men cling fiercely to their prejudices!" he added, with dry humour. "My wife will forgive my outspokenness concerning her father—Miss Brandon's grandfather."

"Oh, yes!" Katherine Minton agreed, with a twinkle in her eyes. "As to old men and prejudices, perchance I shall find such fault in my own husband, one day, Mr. York!" she added pertly.

Sir Jessel laughed good-humouredly. Obviously, he adored his pretty wife.

Katherine told Philip, frankly, that there was little she could say concerning her sister, except that they had been good friends as children, and she had missed her sorely after her runaway marriage. Mary had contacted her very infrequently, after the marriage, and messages had been even more few and far between after she had reached Australia; the last had been to tell her of the birth of Anne.

"And so you see," Sir Jessel said, at the conclusion of his wife's tale, "we are curious to know how your path and Anne's have crossed. Your solicitors would, naturally, say little, but we persuaded them to divulge your whereabouts; I make no apology for our persistence. My wife is most anxious to have news of her niece, and to know all the circumstances; hence our arrival today, without announcement."

"That was my doing," Katherine said calmly. "Nothing would satisfy me but that we should come to see you with all speed. I understand that Anne is staying here, as your guest."

"She was," Philip said heavily, "when I first communicated with my solicitors, asking them to endeavour to trace you; since then much has happened."

He recounted the story that had begun when he had set foot in Sydney; omitting only from his tale any reference to a liaison between Richard and Anne since Richard's marriage. Watching his face, Katherine thought: he loves her to distraction. I am glad. He is a man one would trust; I do not like the sound of Richard Roxton at all.

"*Taroola*," Sir Jessel said softly. "A strange name for a mother to wish to give her child."

"I much prefer Anne," Philip agreed. "It has a sound of gentle dignity. Taroola is a wild, strange name."

Yet in some ways it sat well upon her, he thought; she was a strange, proud, unusual woman.

"Have you no idea where Miss Brandon may have gone?" Philip asked. "For *I* know only that she is in London."

Katherine looked thoughtful, shaking her head; it

was not until they had finished tea, that she snapped her fingers and cried suddenly:

"Something has occurred to me, Mr. York! Mary spoke of a woman called Ellen Wells, who was a childhood friend of James, and had promised to help them to elope; but Ellen, it seems, made a whirlwind marriage herself, with a man named—let me see—ah, I have it! Simon *Chantry!* A rogue who relieved her of a small fortune, and left her near penniless. Mary wrote and told me that James had heard from Ellen, who was not a woman to sit and bemoan her fate: she opened a kind of boarding school for young ladies, somewhere in South London! We may be wrong; but should we not try to seek Anne there? It is possible she may have gone to her, for James was as fond of Ellen as though she was his sister!"

Philip drew a deep breath.

"Accept my hospitality for this night," he said, "then you can begin your journey early in the morning."

Thanking him, Jessel Minton said unexpectedly:

"Will you not accompany us, sir?"

"I do not think Miss Brandon will find my presence necessary," Philip said stiffly.

"Indeed, I am sure she will!" Katherine said eagerly, "for you have been most kind to her. I am hoping that if we find her we can persuade her to return with us—or at least to visit us, for we are her relatives and have no part in the quarrel between our father and James Brandon's father."

He knew he wanted to go; more than anything in the world. Let her rebuff him, reject him, if she would, he thought recklessly. He did not care! It was possible, of course, that the Mintons were wrong, and Anne was not with Ellen Chantry; but he would have sacrificed everything he possessed simply to see her again, he realized. The strength of his own feelings staggered him; but he said quietly:

"Very well. I will come with you."

Later that night, alone with her husband, Katherine said:

"I like him. A man of honour whom I would trust implicitly. And he loves Anne more than his very life!"

Jessel's eyebrows rose.

"Has he confided this to you?"

"No; he is not a man to do so. It is something I can see when I look at his face, and hear when he speaks of her."

"Women's fancies!" Jessel shook his head, laughing, but conceded: "Though it might well be true! I like him myself; but she sounds a headstrong young woman, like her father, one who will make up her own mind. Ah, there's the best match of all, between two mettlesome spirits, eh, Katy!" He chucked her under the chin, smiling wickedly.

The morning was steel-grey, the dawn came reluctantly. It had not snowed heavily, Philip realized thankfully; a heavy fall would have made the roads impassable, or, at best, dangerous. As it was, their long journey would take them more than a day, and they would have to put up at an Inn for the night.

He had made his preparations early; he stood in his room, looking towards Roxton Park, and wondering how Richard had fared throughout the long night. He was seriously perturbed about his cousin; Esther should not delay calling a physician, he thought. He would summon one himself, when he was in London. If severe weather set in within the next week or two, it would be much more difficult to bring a man down from London, and Richard's condition warranted no delay. There was not time to tell Esther what he intended to do, he realized; he would send a servant, with a message, before he left for London.

He looked at the hills, all bridal-veiled, and the still trees, naked in the cold morning air; a plume of smoke curled from a nearby chimney; the world seemed to ring with the hollow sound of frost, and, in spite of the warmth of the house, his fingers felt numb. He wondered whether or not Anne would be at his journey's end; and hoped, passionately, that she would be.

Ellen was dozing alone in her parlour; the intricate piece of crochet that had taxed her brain and fingers, together with the heat of the fire, had made her sleepy. When Lallie announced that there were visitors for her, she awoke with a start, hastily adjusting her lace cap, and pulling at her skirts.

"Who are they, Lallie? Parents? No, all my young ladies have gone home for the Christmas holidays. Who, then? Ah, you stupid girl, you did not think to ask. How many times must I tell you. . . ."

They heard the soft voice grumbling long before Ellen reached them; she blinked at them flushed, pushing back straying wisps of hair with nervous fingers.

"Ellen!" said Katherine delightedly. "Ellen Wells! You played with James, though we were not allowed to; and your mama lived in the big house on the hill. . . ."

"Kate Wilton!" Ellen cried, amazed. *"Kate . . . !"*

She looked at them as though she could not believe her eyes; Jessel Minton made the introductions and explained the purpose of their visit. They had been enquiring as to Ellen's whereabouts and not expected to find her so easily.

It was Philip who asked sharply:

"Is Miss Brandon here? Tell me . . . ?"

"Anne?" Ellen sighed. "Yes. She has been with me many weeks. I suppose you are come to take her away? I shall miss her sadly, indeed, for she has been thoughtful and kind and has worked hard; and, if that was not enough, she has been out and about on many an errand of mercy for those less fortunate than herself. She is out on such an errand now; come—you look cold and weary." She looked at Philip, and thought that Anne had been foolish to run away from the kindness of such a man as this. She looked at Katherine, feeling a sadness for times past, for the old, happy days. Katherine smiled and said firmly:

"Dear Ellen, now that we have found you—and I confess I should have sought you long since, for I thought of you often—we shall see to it that we do not lose sight of one another; and now, if you offer us the warmth of your hearth and some hot food, we shall accept most gratefully!"

So it was that Taroola came upon them all, some time later, when she returned, chilled and tired; she pushed open the door of Ellen's room, puzzled by the unaccustomed sound of many voices; and then stood as though frozen, seeing only Philip, tall, darkly handsome, a moment's unguarded feeling in his face at the sight of her there, clad in the long, dark cloak, its hood slipping from her shining hair.

Katherine went to her at once before Ellen had time to announce the identity of her visitors.

"Anne, my dear! I am your Aunt Katherine, your mother's younger sister, and this is my husband, Jessel."

Taroola stared at her, for a moment, saying nothing, remembering how angry she had been when Philip told her that he was trying to trace her relatives. She was so tall that Katherine had to stand on tiptoe to kiss her, which she did, quite unselfconsciously.

"You are not at all like your mother, except for your hair!" Katherine told her frankly. "My dear child, you cannot know what a joy it is to have found you. Family quarrels between your grandfather and your father's father are nothing to us. We have thought of you, often, and never expected to see you. You have cousins, my dear; Jessel and I have three children. A ready-made family! Is that not a splendid thing, after believing yourself to be alone in the world? And your father's family, I believe, also wish to have news of you!"

For a moment, Taroola stood silent; but nothing could have crumbled her defences more surely than the sincerely spoken speech. Philip saw the glitter of tears in the lovely eyes, as she bent her head to return her Aunt's kiss. She had not realized, until her stay in London, how lonely she had been, how lost she had felt. In spite of her pride, her independence, she knew a sudden feeling of kinship with these people that was both sweet and strange.

Ellen complained loudly that she did not want to part with Taroola; Katherine laughed, and said Ellen and Taroola must come to Kent to stay with them, and Jessel said that their two sons and daughter would be delighted with their new cousin. In the midst of all the talk and commotion, Taroola looked across the room, acutely aware of Philip watching her, the outsider at the family scene. She went across to him and said formally:

"You have news of both Russington and Roxton, I am sure?"

"Not good news, so far as Roxton is concerned. Richard is very ill," he told her abruptly. He saw the whiteness of her face, the troubled look in her eyes as he recounted the story of the strange illness that plagued Richard.

"I must see him!" she insisted.

There was silence in the room, save for the hiss of flames between the logs, and the voice of Ellen's clock. So she was still fathoms deep in love with Richard, Philip thought bitterly!

Taroola turned towards her Aunt, who stood silent, watching her thoughtfully.

"I have some affection for Richard," she said, with complete candour. "At one time I believed I would marry him, but it was not to be. Philip, no doubt, has told you the story. I *cannot* leave him, thus, so desperately ill, without seeing him once more! Afterwards, I promise, I will come to stay with you."

Katherine looked disappointed; she had hoped to take her new-found niece home with her; but she understood, and nodded.

"We hope you will come to us for Christmas, my dear," she said. "That is but three weeks from now; you know how welcome you will be."

Before leaving London, Philip arranged for a physician, a man well known for his skill in diagnosing internal disorders, to be driven down to Roxton Park a few days after his own departure with Taroola.

She felt exhausted by the events of the last few days; she had grown used to her life in London and would miss Ellen. Ellen had accepted the invitation to spend Christmas in Kent, much to Katherine's joy. There was the discovery that she had quite a number of aunts, uncles and cousins; the fact that she had been left a great deal of money, which Jessel had told her when they were alone. She did not want it, she thought; she would give it away to those who had more need of it. The one thought uppermost in her mind was that Richard was ill, for, although she no longer loved him with all the passion she had once known, he still meant a great deal to her.

She asked Philip for details, as the coach threaded its way out of London on the road to the west; he told her all that he knew, keeping back nothing.

"*You* have seen Richard recently!" he said curtly.

"Yes," she admitted.

Jealousy bit deeply into him.

"He spent three days here with you; Esther had no knowledge of his whereabouts. It was unforgivable that he should humiliate his wife so!"

"I spent but an evening with Richard!" she corrected angrily. "We dined together, no more! I did not know that his wife was unaware of his absence!"

Philip's black brows drew together.

"Why did he come to you!"

Her head tilted with proud defiance. "I wrote to Richard's mother! She did not receive my letter. *Esther* took it, and wrote a reply, pretending that it had come from Lady Eleanor!" she declared scornfully.

He looked at her warily.

"Why did you write to Lady Eleanor?"

"That does not concern you!" she replied swiftly.

He leant forward, in the jolting swaying carriage, and held her hands firmly in his.

"It may be important, Anne. There are strange things that I do not understand. Eleanor, for instance, tells me a garbled tale of a package hidden by Esther in the old Nursery that she found and gave into your keeping."

"It is true that Lady Eleanor gave me a package to keep for her."

"What did it contain?" he wanted to know.

She shook her head, her face guarded and withdrawn.

"That I shall not tell you. I destroyed it. Richard came to me because he was concerned about it. There is no more to say." Gently, but firmly, she drew her hands away, and averted her gaze, staring out of the window, at the white world, hazed with the fog that would make travelling difficult.

He felt uneasy about Esther; why had she not given Lady Eleanor the letter intended for her? What had been so important about the package to send Richard hotfoot to London? In vain, he tried to draw Taroola out, but she would not talk of it; she had been speaking the truth, he thought, when she said she had not spent three days with Richard. She had faced him clearly and honestly, and he had known that she did not lie.

They stayed overnight at a small Inn; Taroola was quiet and retired to her own room, pleading a headache, after they had dined. A sense of foreboding troubled her; she was anxious to be at Roxton.

They made an early start next morning; Philip and

Taroola spoke little, and the overwhelming longing he felt for her was intensified by their close proximity in the carriage. Sometimes, she slept, and seeing the lines of strain and weariness on her face, he felt tremendous compassion for her; but he knew she would have none of him. She spoke of her life at Ellen's, the kindness Ellen had shown her, the invitation to spend Christmas at Minton Hall with her relations; she asked after Lady Eleanor, and never mentioned Richard at all—the one person who most occupied her thoughts, Philip reflected ironically.

As they penetrated deeper into the West Country, Philip noticed that there had been heavier falls of snow since they had left Roxton. Their progress was slow, and both he and Taroola chafed at the delay; the dusk was coming down again over the cold white fields as they reached the road into Quinton St. John. He sighed with relief; Taroola gathered her cloak around her and shivered, as though with an awareness of disaster.

"We are almost there," she murmured.

"And you will be with Richard," he said shortly. "I do not imagine that Esther will welcome you; the position is a delicate one, for she knows that there was much feeling between you and Richard."

Taroola lifted a quiet face to his; her eyes were intensely blue, and he thought she had never looked so beautiful; she reminded him of an old painting of the Madonna that had been his father's and still hung in the study at Russington.

"There has, as you say, been much feeling between Richard and myself," she agreed calmly. "That was in days past; what is left is some small affection for remembrance of those days, compassion, an awareness I cannot explain that I must go to him; but no more than that, so you need feel no anxiety on Esther's behalf. I have assured you that I have never been Richard's mistress even though I am not called upon to account to you for my actions, Philip. Sufficient that I have done nothing of which I am ashamed and so I do not fear to meet Esther Roxton."

Philip was silent; the challenge in her voice and face exhilarated him like the icy wind sweeping over the snowy fields. What a woman with whom to share one's life, he thought! Impulsive, passionate, candid; a woman without coyness or other feminine wiles.

They rounded the last corner before Roxton, and suddenly all was confusion. There were people in the road leading to the gates, shouting and pointing, running almost under the feet of the horses. The driver pulled up sharply within yards of the gates. Philip and Taroola climbed down from the carriage and stared ahead, in horror.

The great grey bulk of Roxton Park was crouched against a background of white hills and stark trees; there were pinpoints of light in some of the lower rooms, there was running and shouting here, too; it was to the upper windows in the east wing that they both looked. In that wing was Richard's room; and no pinpoint of light glimmered there, beside the sick-bed. The window was lit from within by a menacing orange glow of fire; even as they looked, little tongues of flame licked hungrily at the heavy curtains in the window.

"My God!" Philip cried. "The house is afire! Quickly . . . !"

CHAPTER TEN

"Hurry!" Philip cried to the driver, as they hastened back into the carriage.

The driver urged the horses forward, through the gates, along the drive to the house; the great front door was wide open, and one of the servants dashed out, as Taroola and Philip stepped down from the carriage.

"What happened?" Philip demanded.

"Fire in the master's room, sir! No one knows how it began. They are making a chain, bringing the buckets of water up from the kitchen!" the man cried.

"Sir Richard—" Taroola began fearfully.

"He is out of danger, ma'am, thanks to his mother—"

Taroola did not wait for details; she ran into the house; smoke was drifting down the shallow curve of the staircase; there was a smell of burning wood, and the acrid taste of charred fabric in her nostrils; she pushed past the hurrying servants, hearing the sharp crackle of flames away to her left, as she reached the first floor. Richard was safe, she thought thankfully! But where was he? She looked left and right, and then she saw him at the far end of the Picture Gallery being lifted by the servants and carried down the stairs at the back of the house; behind the servants was Eleanor, hurrying them forward, her dishevelled hair falling about her grimy face.

Taroola ran after Eleanor and caught at her arm.

"Richard?" she whispered. "Is he all right?"

"Yes, thank God!" Eleanor cried. "I was just in time!"

"Where is Esther?" Taroola asked.

Eleanor turned a ravaged face towards Taroola, her eyes full of hatred.

"Dead for all I know or care!" she whispered fiercely. "She tried to kill my son!"

All that afternoon, Eleanor had been uneasy, for no accountable reason. Beneath her uneasiness, burned a slow-smouldering resentment against Esther. It was Esther who locked her in her room and kept the servants from her with tales that she was resting, that Hawkins was attending to all her wants. Eleanor had begun to hate Hawkins, who was rough and sharp with her when she brought her food, and locked the door behind her after each visit. In vain, Eleanor hammered on the door and cried out to Hawkins to release her, sobbing that Sir Thomas would punish her when he returned; the room she occupied, to which Esther had recently moved her, was in the unfrequented wing of the house near Richard's old Nursery. And so, Eleanor's resentment grew, and fermented within her. Once a day she was allowed to see Richard, and that was when Esther brought up the bowl of soup or gruel that comprised his evening meal; then the ritual was always the same—Hawkins let her out, and took her along to the sick room, where Esther waited outside, with the tray ready. Eleanor was allowed to take the tray into Richard, to sit by him and coax him to eat or drink a little; he turned his head away, complaining that he did not want it, that Esther was poisoning him, but he was often too weak to resist when Eleanor spooned a little of the liquid into his mouth, at Esther's promptings. He would lie there, hatred in his eyes as he glared at Esther; and for the last two days, Eleanor had refused to force the meal upon him, much to the annoyance of Esther, who had boxed her ears and called her a troublesome, mischievous old woman. As a punishment, Eleanor had been locked in her room without light or heat; in the bitter weather, she had sat alone in the darkness, chilled to the bone, miserable and bewildered; and all the time the anger had burned, deep and slow-mounting, within her.

This afternoon, matters had come to a head; when Hawkins had brought her meagre tea, Eleanor's resentment had suddenly exploded into violence; she pushed the tray angrily away, taking the maid by surprise and causing her to stumble. She was a large, heavily-built woman, and as she fell she struck her head on the corner of the big iron fender. The blow stunned her, and while she lay there Eleanor ran from the room, locking the door behind her, feeling a heady sense of freedom.

She had gone to the Nursery; standing there, in the

dusty, quiet room, remembering the day she had heard
Esther talking to Augustus Peach. Every small detail
had come back to her, every word of their conversation, and the anger flowed hotly through her again. Esther had brought some trouble upon her beloved son,
Richard; Esther should suffer for that, she thought bitterly. She had made her way to the room where
Richard lay, and where Esther sat beside him, hour after hour, a picture of selfless devotion, concerned only
for her sick husband. Eleanor had watched the servants
coming and going, and when the way was clear, she
had edged carefully towards the door of Richard's
room, slowly, quietly, turning the handle.

Esther sat with her back to the door, in a high,
winged chair facing the bed in which Richard lay
against his pillows, his face grey and full of pain;
though dusk was approaching, the curtains were not
yet drawn, nor the candles lighted in their sconces; the
room was warmed by the red glow of a fire banked
high. There was the medicine that the physician had
ordered, by Richard's bed; his face was turned towards
the window, his eyes closed; and, as Eleanor watched,
Esther poured a measure of the medicine into a cup,
took a tiny packet from the bodice of her dress and
tipped a small quantity of white powder into the medicine. It was swiftly and neatly done; then she stirred it
carefully; got up, put a taper to the heart of the fire,
and lit the candles from it. Finally, she roused the sleeping Richard, with a shake so gentle that it might have
come from a loving hand rather than of a woman who
hated him and was watching him die with such
pleasure.

"Come, Richard," she said softly. "It is time for you
to take your medicine."

Through the narrow crack she had made by opening
the door a couple of inches, Eleanor watched Richard
shake his head, his eyes still closed.

"I take nothing from your hands," he whispered.

"Nothing! Whatever *you* give me is tainted with poison!" A spasm of pain twisted his face suddenly.

She put a soothing hand on his forehead.

"Richard, what wild nonsense is this! Very well, so you will not take your medicine!" She laughed softly, her green eyes glowing as she bent over him. "It matters little, now, my love!" she whispered, so softly that Eleanor had to listen intently to catch the words. "Do you know what your foolish cousin Philip had planned to do? He is going to have another physician come to see you, to find out what ails you. A clever and famous man from London!"

"Then he will discover the mischief you have done to me!" Richard cried, with a flash of spirit.

Esther gave a gentle sigh and shook her head.

"No, my dearest," she said, almost matter-of-factly. "You will not be here, when the great man comes from London; it will all be over for you then, my poor Richard!"

"How?" he demanded fearfully. *"How?"*

Esther was still smiling, as she went across and drew the curtains; in that moment, her half-formulated plan crystallized. She picked up the sconce and deliberately let candle-grease drip over the coverlet. Softly, she explained:

"An *accident,* my love! Just as I had left the room and gone in search of a servant you tried to get from your bed and overturned the candles! Who will hear you cries, until it is too late? I have told the servants not to come near, unless I summon them, for fear of disturbing you. When the physician comes, it will be too late—there will be nothing to *find!"* Swiftly, she pulled back the coverlets, and pulled Richard, weakly protesting, from the bed, letting him fall to the floor, and, at the same time, she slowly and deliberately tipped the candle in its silver sconce, on to the bed.

Eleanor began to scream; a high-pitched, terrified scream that startled the servants downstairs; Esther turned, and jumped violently. For the first time in her life, she was caught off guard; as she hesitated, Eleanor thrust past her, and with a strength that met the needs of the moment, she dragged Richard clear of the room; already, the flames from the candle were licking the coverlets, and the thin bed-drapes, with hungry anticipation. But the fire that would have destroyed all evidence of what Esther had done to Richard had not touched him, after all; and, in the wake of Eleanor's screams, the servants came running upstairs, as Esther stood irresolute. In sudden panic, hearing their footsteps and voices, she made as though to beat the flames out with her hands, wildly pulling covers from the bed, as the burning drapes fell around her; at least, they would think she had tried to help Eleanor to quench the fire, she thought, as she ran from the room, and called to them to bring up buckets of water.

But the kitchen and the pumps were far enough from the upper floor, for it to be a journey, and the fire caught hungrily at soft fabrics and old timbers. The servants panicked; Esther, her thoughts only of her son, hurried to the Nursery and snatched him up, hustling the nursemaid out.

Eleanor dragged Richard to the far end of the Picture Gallery, sobbing, distracted, crying to the servants to help her; thus, Taroola found her, some time later, as two of them bundled Richard into blankets, and carried him from the upper floor, where the flames now crackled fiercely in the face of the pitifully inadequate buckets of water tossed at it; a pall of smoke drifted with the flames, making Taroola cough and splutter. Philip was by her side, in a matter of moments; weakly, she leant against him.

"Richard is safe," she murmured. "They have carried him out of harm's way, and his mother is with him. I have not seen Esther."

"It is not safe to stay!" Philip cried. "Go, Anne! The servants are panicking! If I can restore them to some kind of order, then we can make a human chain of buckets, though I fear this fire is too much for us!"

She nodded, unwilling to leave him; but the voice of the fire crackled more loudly, and sparks were mingled with the smoke that rolled towards them. The servants were retreating, helpless, in the face of the suffocating smoke and intense heat that met them like an implacable wall.

At that moment, Esther, having seen her son safely into the arms of the nursemaid, came back into the house, full of blind, searing fury that she had been cheated. How much had Eleanor heard? Ah, but what did it matter? Anything, *she* said could easily be dismissed as the senile babblings of a demented woman. How had Eleanor got out of her room? *Hawkins,* she thought! The old Nursery wing! She shrugged; well, it was nothing to do with HER, she reflected; if Hawkins had been foolish enough to let herself be trapped there.

The smoke was so thick she could scarcely see; the flames were licking along the gallery towards the staircase, and she suddenly saw Philip, his arm around Taroola. Fury and despair overwhelmed her; she had not expected to see them here, *now*.

"Come down!" she screamed. "The whole house is burning!"

"The back stairs!" Philip cried, pointing towards them; she neither heard his words, nor saw the gesture. She began to run up the great central staircase, shouting wildly at him; she was halfway up, when she tripped and fell, rolling over and over, reaching the bottom as part of the fiercely blazing balustrade collapsed on her.

Horrified, Philip raced down the stairs, Taroola just behind him; Esther lay on her broken back, her great green eyes staring at him, the lower half of her body blossoming into flames where the burning wooden rail had struck her and lay across her legs.

Philip pulled off his cloak and tried to beat out the

flames; but they caught the flimsy stuff of the shawl she had thrown around her, and she began to scream, as he tried to pull away the shawl, and lift the wooden rail.

Desperately, he dragged her out through the hall into the snow, rolling her over and over in the cold whiteness of it; but the flames that had singed her hair and her face, had also burnt her arms and her legs so badly that she still screamed and moaned, and through her agony was threaded strange words and phrases that made no sense to him until long after.

"Philip! Ah, my love, you are back . . . ! It is all over, Richard is dead . . . and you and I . . ." the words died into a scream, rose again on the thin air; Taroola, crouching beside her, listened in horror.

"We shall be wed, Philip . . . it is all over, my dearest . . . God, how I have hated him . . . and that whining fool of a mother . . . nothing to stop us both, now . . . nothing for the physician but a burned corpse!" She started to laugh, a thin, dreadful sound that melted into screams; and then there was silence. . . .

Taroola began to weep, slow, bitter tears, kneeling beside Esther, in the snow. Gently, Philip put his arms around her. Behind them in the gathering darkness, the fire spat and crackled, as though with sullen fury against the people who had lived in the house, destroying it with hungry fingers . . .

Though Philip took charge of the situation coolly and courageously, the fire had gained too great a hold for the frightened servants to bring it under control, and by morning, the entire upper floor of the house was gutted, a blackened, crumbling shell, the staircase destroyed and much of the lower floor badly damaged.

Esther was dead; Philip laid her in the drawing-room, covering her with his own cloak. Hawkins had escaped death by jumping from the window, breaking several bones, but otherwise unharmed. The hysterical nursemaid had fled the scene, leaving the child to run screaming in search of his mother; and no one had seen her; Philip sent the lodgekeeper's wife to Russington to hand Sebastian over to Nanny Gaunt's care. Then he supervised the removal of Richard and his mother to Russington, in the care of a couple of servants; finally, he turned to Taroola, standing beside him; her face grimy and weary, her hair long and flying loose as he had first seen it on a sunny day in Australia. He put a hand gently on her arm.

"Go to Russington," he said gently. "There is much you can do there; Nanny Gaunt will be glad of your help."

She went without demur, only bidding him have a thought for his own safety; he smiled at her, and, long afterwards, she remembered the tender quality of his smile.

There was, as he had predicted, much to be done at Russington; Richard was exhausted and hardly conscious. A bewildered Eleanor was coaxed to bed by a more kindly servant than ever Hawkins had been. Taroola put the frightened, screaming Sebastian to bed, with a mixture of firmness and gentleness that effectively cut short his tantrums and soothed his fears.

Nanny Gaunt treated Richard, as though he, too, was a child; she got him to bed, and gave him broth which he took readily. Then he asked for Taroola. . . .

She was tired; she had shed her cloak, but her dress was crumpled and dirty, and her hair still awry; she came to the side of the bed, and looked down at Richard, grown thin and grey and looking so much older than the carefree, bright-haired young man who had whispered in her ear and kissed her and held her hands long ago; she felt pain and sadness for the past, but she managed to smile, as he looked up at her.

"Sit down," he said, pointing to the chair by the bed. "Are all the servants gone?" She nodded, and he said:

"There are things I must tell you."

"Not tonight, Richard," she said gently. "For now you are weary. Tell me tomorrow, when you are rested."

Pain crumpled his face for a moment, but he shook his head; small beads of perspiration lay along his upper lip.

"I must tell you tonight, Taroola, before I sleep. I can no longer keep this burden of knowledge to myself; and when Philip comes, *you* will tell *him* my story. . . ."

She sat down and caught hold of the hand that reached for hers; holding it firmly, as though to give him strength.

"The pardon," he said. "The one Philip brought to set me free. My father bought it; better he had never done so! Better I had still been a convict. But—my father—when I was convicted . . ." The voice died away, rose again, went on with difficulty, ". . . it was monstrous blow to him . . . his only son . . . he believed me innocent, knew that the other man with me was Matthew Warby. Matthew and I both planned the robbery . . . the jewels . . ." he sighed. "Matthew got the jewels . . . shipped them abroad . . . was paid a handsome sum for them. . . ."

"And you killed the man who was carrying the jewels," Taroola said gently. "Your eyes answered me when I asked that question in London."

"Yes, I killed him," Richard said flatly. "Matthew took the jewels . . . and fled . . . I was transported, nothing *proved* . . . when I returned home, my father told me he had spent many weary months and a great fortune searching for Matthew Warby; and, eventually, he found him—ill, with very little time to live. My father told me when I came home that he knew his only chance of ever seeing me again was to get a confession from Warby."

"So he paid him for one?" Taroola asked. "Is *that* what he did?"

Richard nodded.

"A very great deal of money. Matthew drove a hard bargain . . . and he made conditions. My father must sign a statement saying that he had agreed to hand over the money immediately Matthew had confessed; Matthew, knowing he was dying, said he would send for my father and the magistrate, as soon as he realized his time had come, and make a false confession, stating that he had killed the messenger for the jewels. It would not matter to him, then, he said; they would not trouble to take a dying man to prison to await trial."

"If he was dying," Taroola asked, "why did he need the money?"

The smile on Richard's lips was bitter and sardonic; after several seconds of silence, he said tiredly:

"Matthew was an old man. His greatest prize was a wife, many years younger than him. Esther Warby."

Taroola drew a long, incredulous breath; the room was so quiet that she could count her heart's hammer-strokes. Richard's smile was cynical.

"Esther had little pleasure from an old man . . . the child, Sebastian . . ."

"It was yours," Taroola said softly. "Is that not what you are trying to say to me?"

He nodded and closed his eyes, turning his face from her, as though he could not meet her glance. Her fingers tightened over his.

"It does not matter, now, Richard," she assured him, quietly. "Did Matthew know that the child was yours?"

Richard shook his head weakly.

"No . . ." He spoke as though he had little breath to spare. "Had he known . . . he would not have confessed, even to have given Esther such a bounty . . . think he would have killed her . . . nor did my father know about the child. . . ."

Taroola sat silent in the firelight; outside, a wind was rising, fretting sadly at the walls of the house, as though it wanted to come in, and warm itself by the fire; she sighed, thinking how strange were the ways of men and the world. Richard's father had made Richard's mistress rich; but that was not all the story, she knew. She looked down at Richard, with his grey face, and carefully wiped the perspiration from his forehead with her kerchief.

"Matthew told Esther, his wife, the story of the confession and the money that was to be paid—is that so, Richard?" she asked; and he nodded. He seemed utterly spent, but he forced the words on, as though he could no longer bear to keep them locked inside of him.

"Matthew cheated . . . God, how he cheated! He wrote out a statement, saying that he had been bribed to make false confession . . . gave it to Esther, with the damning piece of paper, signed by my father, agreeing to hand over the money . . . Matthew hated me. God knows why . . . perhaps he suspected Esther and me . . . I know not; but Esther says he told her that as soon as I was back at Roxton, she was to take the evidence to the authorities . . . I would be hanged at Tyburn . . . it was what he wanted, though he would not be there to see it . . . but she was to do it for him . . . might have been better for me if she had . . . !" He groaned with sudden pain, and added, with difficulty:

"She came to Quinton St. John . . . saw Roxton Park, and changed her plans . . . thought it a better idea to become Lady Roxton . . . she believed I was wealthy!" He grimaced, a travesty of a smile, as though it was the only horribly funny part of the whole affair. "Bargained with me . . . she had the papers . . . what could I do . . . ? Married her . . . oh, I planned to get rid of her. . . ."

He went on to explain how the papers had been delivered by Mr. Peach, found by his mother, who had not understood the contents, but felt them to be dangerous, and so had handed them to Taroola; the rest,

she already knew. He told her that Esther's plan had
been to denounce him, inherit Roxton for herself and
her son, then marry Philip; deprived of the quick, easy
means of achieving this, she had found another . . . he
did not understand until he remembered something
Bessie had said: *arsenic, to keep the hands white . . .
a woman's secret;* and then she had once said that Esther went shopping, far afield . . . to Apothecaries'
shops. . . .

"Oh, *no,* Richard!" Taroola whispered, on a sharply
indrawn breath.

"It is true," he said dully. "Poison. She brought the
tray, each night, then sent for my mother to feed me
. . . during those few minutes alone she added the
powder . . . so easy . . . I never guessed . . . until today . . . when she knew the Physician was coming and
might discover the truth . . . tried to destroy me . . .
so she set fire to the room, but my mother came. . . ."

He closed his eyes, as though he was very tired. She
sat there, holding his hand, reflecting that she had
never heard such a dreadful tale in her whole life.

The first pale streaks of dawn lay across the cold
Eastern sky when Philip rode home to Russington,
damp, chilled and deathly tired, his hands and face
grimy, his clothing torn. Taroola was waiting for him in
the hall; she had washed and changed her gown and
brushed her hair. He looked at her in surprise.

"Have you not been to bed?" he asked abruptly.

She shook her head.

"I waited for you," she said simply. "Give me your
cloak. I have heated broth, and kept the fire ablaze. I
will bring the broth to you."

He sank wearily on to the little brocaded couch in
the drawing-room, grateful for the warmth and peace
after the long night's battle at Roxton, that he had
barely won.

"Is it over?" she asked fearfully, when she brought
the soup.

"Yes, but little enough is saved, except the ground floor, and those rooms are in a sorry state. How is Richard . . . his mother . . . the child . . . ?"

"Sleeping, all of them. Richard seems a little easier." She sat composedly in front of him, hands folded in her lap. "He told me a strange tale, Philip; do you wish to hear it now, or when you have rested?"

"I will hear it now," he said.

He listened to the whole story in silence; only when she had finished, did he say:

"In Heaven's name, I swear I have never heard of anything more strange! A fantastic tale, indeed!"

"I believe it to be true, Philip."

He stared broodingly into the heart of the fire.

"It is astonishing—such hate and greed in one woman! Poor Richard!" he said, with unexpected compassion. "A macabre story indeed! An old man, doting on his son, indulging him in all things; pledging his honour and paying a vast sum of money because of that very weakness *he* had fostered! Truly does folly beget folly, and weakness foster weakness; better, as Richard himself has truly said, that his father had left him in Australia. And Esther!" He drew a deep breath and shook his head. "Her obsession became madness; but that I was part of that obsession was something I never gave thought to until last night, I swear!"

He looked at her sombrely; Taroola looked away, her heart suddenly agitated. Her pity was for the man who lay so ill in the room upstairs; he had long since forfeited her love, though she had stubbornly turned her face from that truth. *This* man, she knew, could rouse in her a passion that she would give as a woman, not as the untried girl on an Australian sheep station. . . .

"It is possible that Richard has been saved," Philip said, with an effort. "The Physician will see him, as I have arranged; if the effects of the poison have not been too grave, and if he is carefully nursed, he will yet recover, please God! And as there is no longer evidence to convict him of murder, he can live the rest of his life in peace."

Dear Philip, she thought, tenderly! He would give me Richard, because he believes I still care for him; renouncing his own claims in his desire to see me happy. Where could I find a greater love to which to surrender?

She knew it was not the time to tell him the truth; she merely said composedly:

"If you wish, Philip, I will stay and help you with the nursing."

"It will not be necessary," he said quietly. "Nanny Gaunt will be glad to have something to do. Richard's mother needs only kindness and comfort; Sebastian also, will be in Nanny's care for a time, but she has long chafed at inactivity and will welcome being so employed. It would make your relatives happy if you went to them at Christmas, Anne! Your visit will heal old wounds!"

"Yes," she agreed quietly. "Yes, you are right."

Taroola stayed at Russington for another two weeks. During that time, the Physician who came confirmed that Richard had been given progressively large doses of poison; another small packet of the powder such as Eleanor saw her use, had been found tucked inside the bodice of her dress. It was identified as arsenic. Richard, the Physician said, would need very careful nursing. . . .

Eleanor was an unexpected ally; freed from the unhappiness she had known at Roxton, and the unkindness she had suffered at Esther's hand, she helped Nanny Gaunt willingly, and her greatest pleasure was to sit near Richard, ready to attend his wants. Nanny, as Philip had predicted, was happy enough with her hands full. Sebastian accepted with surprising meekness that she would suffer no nonsense in the way of tantrums from him, but would reward good behaviour and treat him with justice.

To Philip fell the added burden of trying to manage affairs on the Roxton Estate, as well as his own commitments. He came to Taroola, as she stood dressed for her journey to Kent, one afternoon just before Christmas. Outside, the white world of December was unutterably peaceful; inside, she created her own warmth and splendour, he thought, beautiful in her furs and rich travelling cloak. She looked serene and he thought that she had never seemed more desirable. With a spasm of pain, deep within him, he realized that her happiness was for Richard's safety and the promise of a future together.

"I hope, indeed, my visit will heal the old wounds; and I will come back in the New Year, Philip, if I may," she said.

"You may stay here as long as you wish. You will naturally desire to be near Richard," he said formally.

"That is not my reason, Philip." She looked at him candidly. "Though I pray that all will go well with him whilst I am away."

"You will marry him when he is recovered," Philip said harshly. "For now there are no obstacles!"

"Indeed you are wrong! *You* once asked me to marry you, Philip! I told you then that I had no heart for a marriage of convenience, for I believed myself still deeply in love with your cousin; but I have known, these many weeks, that I gave him only a girl's first love, untried, not meant to endure. Ah, Philip, you will not make it easy for me, will you?" she cried, cheeks flushed, eyes bright. "Do you not understand? If you asked me to marry you *now* I would answer you differently, and with all my heart!"

He stared at her incredulously for a moment; then he crossed the room and took her hungrily into his arms, his face questioning and searching.

"My love, my dearest love!" he whispered urgently; he put up his hands and his fingers gently travelled over her face, like a blind man exploring beloved contours to reassure himself that they remained unchanged.

"Ah!" he said suddenly. "You *will* change your mind! You will not come back! It is all a dream!"

"How little faith you have!" she protested. "Philip, I care for you as I have cared for no other man!"

"I can scarcely bear to let you go!" he whispered against her hair. "Anne, my dearest! I have wanted to possess you for so many months, I have seen no face but yours. When you went this house seemed to cry out in pain with a despairing loneliness! I will wait, aye, for months, if you will promise to return!"

"I will come back, my beloved!" she promised him, between kisses that made her heart feel as though it was on fire. "In the Spring—the lovely English Spring of which I have heard so much—we shall be wed!"

With that promise, she left him; the loneliness seared him like a fire, but there was no despair in it this time. . . .

Taroola returned to Russington, in the New Year. She had written to Philip, but not informed him of the time of her coming, for she wished to surprise him. Yet, some sixth sense, born of his love for her, alerted all his senses, so that he was waiting when the carriage came through the gates and drove up to the front door. The snow had been cleared along the driveway, but it lay thick still on hedgerows and trees and over the quiet fields beyond the house.

"Anne!" he said softly; he took her hand and led her indoors, sending the servants scurrying for hot tea and food. Her eyes answered his question with gladness and reassurance; but there was something wrong, and she knew it. When they were alone by the fire, she told him, in response to his question, that her Christmas had been happy and she had much to talk of; and then she asked after the welfare of the three who stayed at Russington.

"Anne," he said quietly, "I have sad news for you, my dearest love. Richard died on the last day of the old year. His mother was with him; his end was peaceful and kind. He thanked me for what I had done, and sent a wish to you for happiness all your life. The Physician said that the poison had taken too great a hold on a weakened body; and that Richard had, also, some incurable disease which had not been previously suspected, but which had hastened his end. I am sorry that you return to such unhappy news!"

Her eyes filled with tears; but she smiled, and said quietly:

"I do not think that Richard would have wished to live on, you know, Philip; the burdens his mind bore were too great. Now he is at peace, and I am glad. Has his mother taken it very hardly?"

"Better than I would have believed. She has turned much of her attention to Sebastian, for I have told her he is Richard's son, and she seems to find some comfort in that, as though she had Richard as a child again."

"What will become of them both?" she asked him.

He looked thoughtful.

"It will be many, many months before they can return to Roxton Park. Even so, they are not fitted to live alone there: an old lady, and a young child. I am perturbed about it, though Richard has left his estates to me to manage in trust for the boy."

"We could keep them with us, Philip," she said quietly. "The house is big enough. Eleanor will be happy; the child will grow up here better fitted to face life than ever his father was. Do you not agree? We shall have enough happiness, you and I, to be able to share it with those two, who need it so much."

She held out her arms; he went across to where she sat, pulled her to her feet gently, and held her against him, straining her body to his, with yearning and longing and the passionate tenderness that she had learned to love.

"You are generous, my love!" he whispered. "Very

well! They shall remain here. God, how I have missed you!" he whispered fiercely. "Longed for you so sorely, my dearest. We will not wait for the Spring for our wedding. I *cannot* wait! You talk of sharing our happiness—aye, that we will both do gladly! But I tell you, Anne, you have not yet known what happiness is! There is so much for me to teach you, when we are married!"

"Yes." She bowed her head, in sudden surrender; he thought of the fine, splendid spirit that he would never seek to crush. She would give him all of herself, freely, gladly; he thought of her by his side, his beloved beautiful Anne, forever at Russington with him. A marriage that their grandchildren would speak of with envy, he thought; a gift of passion accepted by each with humility; and a deeper love even than that, transforming all the days of their life together.

"My love," he said softly.

"And you are *my* love—always!" she promised.

The rags-to-riches story of Morris,
star of the 9-Lives cat food
commercials, the feline superstar
millions watch on TV.

MORRIS

An Intimate Biography
by Mary Daniels

"THE ROBERT REDFORD
OF CATDOM"
— New York Daily News

57 photographs
plus
a nude centerfold

Over 80,000 copies sold in hardcover

A DELL BOOK
$1.50
5673-05

At your local bookstore or use this handy coupon for ordering: